Praise for

THE AMAZING MR. MORALITY

"These short stories and a novella explore, with Appel's trademark dark humor, contemporary life and its ethical dilemmas. As in his previous, fine collections, the author draws on his experiences as a physician, attorney, and bioethicist to inform these tales. Another excellent Appel collection of intelligent, humanistic, and witty stories that bite."

—*Kirkus* (starred review)

"Every single story in *The Amazing Mr. Morality* contains a nugget of insight into modern life, and some facet of each story's ending—be it an unexpected twist or a good ironic joke—lingers in the memory long after reading."

—*Foreword Reviews*

"In this collection of disturbing, addictive, provocative stories, the situations bristle with the reach of unrepentant longing and unexpected persistence. Appel's stories never fail to impress; they never fail, period."

—Karen Heuler, author of *The Inner City* and *In Search of Lost Time*

"Accomplished and assured."

—Silas Dent Zobal, author of *The People of the Broken Neck* and *The Inconvenience of the Wings*

"The characters in *The Amazing Mr. Morality* sing like so many sirens, wailing their desires, plotting, misguiding, and deceiving for causes noble and base. With wit and tenderness, Jacob Appel's stories illuminate the awkward truths of what it means to be human."

—Tyrone Jaeger, author of *So Many True Believers*

FEB 2018

JACOB M. APPEL

The **AMAZING MR. MORALITY**

STORIES

VANDALIA PRESS • MORGANTOWN 2018

CONTENTS

-⫷◆⫸-

THE CHILDREN'S LOTTERY

—⫷⫸—

Some of the senior teachers gathered at Finley's Pub each year to watch a live broadcast of the children's lottery, but Oriana Hapley preferred to check the results in the newspaper the next day. She'd been teaching at Foxglove for six years, after all, and not once had their school—or any other school across the city of Creve Coeur—been among the fifty-eight public elementary schools randomly selected during the statewide sweepstakes. According to her husband, Kurt, Oriana's students had a better chance of being snatched off the street by wolves or falling into sinkholes during recess. So Oriana was unprepared to see Foxglove listed on the front page of the *Sentinel* and genuinely shocked, forty minutes later, to discover a crimson envelope affixed to her office door—notice that, in three days' time, a registered pedophile would be visiting her classroom.

Oriana refused to let her surprise distract her from her lesson plan. She was a professional, wasn't she? And today, being a professional meant diagramming sentences and reviewing long division exercises to prepare her third graders for their upcoming placement tests. Anyway, it wasn't as though she'd been the first teacher on the planet to receive a crimson envelope. Yet watching pigtailed Lucy Barber separate her adjectives from her adverbs, and listening as bucktoothed Walt Geiss showed Peter Pozner how to carry over remainders, Oriana couldn't resist imagining what the classroom would feel like when one of the tiny chairs stood empty, after her brood of thirty had been systematically reduced to twenty-nine.

"You look sad, Mrs. Hapley," said Walt. "Are you okay?"

"It's just the weather, Walt. I always feel sad in May." She watered the African violets on the window ledge while she spoke. "It's almost summer already, and I'm going to miss you all."

"Please don't feel sad, Mrs. Hapley." Walt had taken to bringing her flowers each morning, plucked from beds on the walk to his bus stop. "We'll come back to visit next year. Promise. And someday, I'm going to become a teacher too, and we can have classrooms side by side."

"Wouldn't that be wonderful?" agreed Oriana.

They did not inform the students in advance, obviously. Even the parents did not know which specific classroom had been chosen. Long ago, apparently, the families had been afforded an opportunity to say goodbye—but this approach placed too much strain on the children who were passed over, and was ultimately abandoned. Far better, everyone agreed, to avoid unnecessary sniveling.

⸻❖⸻

Oriana's colleagues largely kept their distance. Women who'd chatted with her countless mornings in the faculty lounge now struggled to make small talk—as though uncertain whether to mention the sweepstakes. Only a few of the old-timers dared broach the subject directly. Arnold Cobb, the grizzled assistant principal, poked his head into her classroom during a prep period and said, "They all have to grow up sometime. When you think about things rationally, it shouldn't matter whether it's now or in five years. . . ." *Of course not*, she agreed—although she didn't. "Besides," added Cobb, "the winners manage to readjust. In the end, their lives turn out fine." *I know*, replied Oriana, trying to sound appreciative. *That is what they say. . . .*

Later, during lunch duty, Wilma Lindstrom confided to Oriana, "I've lost three over the years—two back-to-back—and the truth is that it never gets easier." A shudder of grief ran through the first grade teacher's voice; Oriana suspected Wilma had suffered a loss more personal than a student—maybe a nephew or a brother—but this wasn't the sort of confidence one shared at work. "Years later, one boy sent me a card. He'd moved to Albany and owned a hardware shop. The card was perfectly friendly, cheerful—not a word in it about the lottery—yet it broke my heart." She smiled pointedly at Oriana's swollen abdomen. "Of course, I never had children of my own."

By the end of the day, Oriana longed to feel her husband's embrace—to rest her face against the crook of his shoulder and to sob. Unfortunately, Mondays were Kurt's late night at the hospital, so he didn't arrive home until nearly eight o'clock. "I got your message," he said as he stashed his raincoat in the closet. "I'm sorry I didn't have a chance to call from the clinic."

And then she had her arms wrapped around him. He let her lean against his chest as though his body were a pillar, holding his attaché case in one hand. Then he steered her into the kitchen and set about preparing their dinner.

"You think I'm overreacting, don't you?" demanded Oriana.

"Honestly, yes," he said. "It's only one child. Aren't teachers always complaining about their class sizes?" He measured out pasta into a pot while he spoke. "Look at the upside. You'll have more energy to devote to your other students."

"I keep thinking about the parents. How would you feel if your child was carried off to live in a pedophile camp?"

"I'd be disappointed. Who wouldn't?" conceded Kurt. "Probably upset too. But what's the alternative?"

"I don't know. It just seems so unfair."

"Would you rather *lock up* the pedophiles? They did that at one time, you know. They used to put them in prisons alongside murderers and thieves."

"I am well aware of that," snapped Oriana. "And before you start

"I thought you might want some company," said Wilma.

She settled into the plastic-backed chair beside Oriana's desk. The nearest children looked up briefly before returning to their construction.

"I don't know what I want," admitted Oriana.

She'd learned that as long as she kept her tone chipper, she could say anything while the children labored—and they'd remain oblivious to the content.

"Have any of the parents contacted you?" asked Wilma.

Oriana surveyed the classroom—taking note of how Walt Geiss was helping Peter Pozner and Max Pastarnack with the layout of their coliseum. Walt would make a marvelous teacher someday, she knew, if given the opportunity. "I haven't been checking my messages," she said. "I thought I'd wait until afterwards."

Parents had been advised not to phone, but that never stopped them.

"It's the best way," agreed Wilma. "Afterwards is more tolerable."

The veteran teacher adjusted the rings on her bloated fingers.

"I've been in your shoes before," she said. "You're choosing favorites. You're asking yourself which of them you'll miss least."

Oriana hadn't realized she'd been doing this—not until her colleague gave voice to her own thoughts—but it was true. Instantly, she recognized that she'd been appraising each of her students, weighing their value like so much meat at the butcher shop. Now the notion repulsed her. How could anyone place a value on Ernie Willoughby's lisp or the precious gap between Annie Gartner's front teeth?

"It's all right, dear," said Wilma—as though she could sense Oriana's emotional self-lashing. "Don't be hard on yourself. You're not the first girl to imagine you could bargain with a visitor. But trust me. You can't. He'll choose whomever he decides to choose and that will be that."

Wilma reached across the desk blotter and squeezed Oriana's wrist. "You *will* get through this, dear," she said. "But try not to think about it too much. Just do your part and move on." Wilma released Oriana's wrist and rose to her feet. "If you start asking difficult questions, you'll only be hurting yourself."

"No difficult questions," pledged Oriana. "Do my part and move on." And she did her utmost to stick to this commitment. When her sister phoned that evening to wish her luck—her family knew not to ask directly whether she'd received the crimson envelope, but they were as capable as anyone of reading into her silences—Oriana shifted the conversation to routine matters. "Maya Pastarnack is teaching everyone to count to ten in Hungarian," she revealed with pride. "And Walt Geiss wrote this lovely poem about guppies. His gift for language is so sophisticated."

Over dinner, she recited Walt's poem for Kurt.

"It is beautiful," said her husband. "He must have a brilliant teacher."

Oriana laughed nervously. She'd never been comfortable accepting compliments, not even from those closest to her.

"I had nothing to do with it. I don't even teach poetry."

"Modesty, my fine wife," said Kurt, "will get you nowhere."

Her husband reached into the pocket of his slacks and produced a slender turquoise box. An instant later, Oriana found herself confronted with the most gorgeous lady's wristwatch—the prohibitively expensive, platinum and ivory wristwatch that she'd admired months earlier in the display window at Brigander's.

"Read the inscription," urged Kurt.

She'd expected a romantic phrase. The words *World's Greatest Teacher* hit her hard—more like a warning than a comfort.

-««•»»-

The pedophile arrived at seven-thirty, in an official limousine, just as the first students were clambering down from their busses. Whichever child won the sweepstakes, Oriana understood, would depart with him in the same vehicle. During a previous era, the selection had taken a full week—with the visitors voting on their choice. Even earlier, the winner had been drawn randomly from among the top vote getters, giving the enterprise its name. Over the decades, the process had been streamlined.

"I'm David," said the pedophile, extending his hand. "Glad to meet you."

David appeared no different than numerous other strangers she might encounter in the neighborhood: a broad-shouldered, lantern-jawed fellow in his forties with a shock of chestnut hair and a neatly trimmed chevron mustache. He was handsome, Oriana acknowledged to herself—even sexy—and his voice sounded surprisingly kind. If not for the fact that he lived in a pedophile colony and would soon carry off one of her charges, he seemed the sort of person she'd welcome onto her block.

Oriana shook his hand. She did not wish to seem rude.

David followed her down the corridor into her classroom.

"Pyramids," he declared when he spotted the students' creations. "I was fascinated by the giant pyramids when I was in third grade."

"We're halfway through a module on ancient history," explained Oriana. "They're working in teams."

"I hope I won't be disrupting your lesson too much," said David—and he sounded sincerely apologetic. "I suppose it might be hard on a team to lose a member in the middle of a project."

"We'll do the best we can," replied Oriana. And for no good reason, she added, "You might be surprised at how resilient children can be at this age."

"Children never cease to surprise me," he answered.

David drifted around the classroom, examining the papier-mâché masonry more closely. Soon the children started appearing, fortified with their brown-bag lunches, their galoshes, their backpacks full of whiteout and rubber cement and paperclips. Oriana helped Lucy Barber remove her willowy arms from her windbreaker. Walt Geiss presented her with a bouquet of mangled forsythia.

"Please don't mind me," said David, sliding into an undersized chair beside the flagpole. "I'll sit here and try to be as unobtrusive as possible."

Oriana shut the classroom door, blocking out the exterior world.

"We have a visitor this morning," announced Oriana. "Mr. David."

And her charges rose for the Pledge of Alliance, as they did every morning.

‑‑«‹«•›»›‑

The pedophile stayed true to his promise and didn't meddle with her teaching. That didn't prevent Oriana from following his eyes with her own—from speculating at the machinations behind his placid smile. Once, when Naomi Hager asked about the difference between silver and mica, he flashed a full-fledged grin, and the notion seized Oriana that she might kill him before he rendered his choice. That made absolutely no sense, of course. Not rationally. She'd go to prison, while her innocent charges would face another lottery, and a blameless man—a man whose only "crime" in life was to have been born a pedophile—would die for nothing. "Mica and silver can look the same," she explained to Naomi, "but silver is much more valuable."

At recess, the other teachers gave Oriana a wide berth. Even Wilma Lindstrom stayed clear of her, offering only an encouraging nod from a distance. Overhead, a clear white sun had burnt off the early morning haze. Catbirds and warblers sang to each other through the undergrowth. Deep inside her own body, Oriana felt the baby shifting his legs, testing the confines of his shell. Once, he delivered a solid blow, pounding her womb for his freedom. She had little choice but to talk with the pedophile, who'd accompanied her to the cusp of the playground.

"That boy with the buck teeth," said David. "What's his name?"

Her gaze trailed his across the sandpit. Walt Geiss and Luke Sestito drew diagrams in the wet earth with sticks; Peter Pozner looked on from the knee-high parapet.

"I thought they gave you a roster with photos," said Oriana.

"If only," answered the pedophile. "This is the State Board of Education we're dealing with here. It's a miracle they sent the limo on the right day."

Oriana also knew how it felt to fight the state bureaucracy, but she refused to bond with the pedophile over his experience. David popped a

"Seven. I'm due in June."

He stepped toward her. "May I?" he asked.

A moment elapsed before she realized that he wanted to touch her belly. Oriana suppressed a yearning to flee—to abandon her visitor and accept the consequences, whatever they might be. But she also sensed herself nodding, letting the man place his broad palm against her dress. His touch scalded like a brand.

"Boy or girl?" he asked.

"We don't know yet," she lied.

After seconds that lasted for hours, he removed his hand. The pedophile was beaming, seemingly oblivious to her horror.

"I've decided," he said. "I'll take the troublemaker. Geiss."

"*Walt Geiss?* Are you sure?"

"He's obviously not contributing much here," replied the pedophile. "Maybe a change of environment will do him some good."

-《《◆》》-

Once the losing children had been loaded onto their busses, Oriana escorted Walt Geiss back to her classroom. In other districts, the handover occurred in the principal's office, under the supervision of multiple administrators, but Arnold Cobb had pioneered a more intimate approach, one less liable to provoke excess trauma. The assistant principal remained on site, along with a nurse and a psychologist, to address any unforeseen emergences. Fortunately, Walt hadn't seemed fazed when Oriana asked him to stay after school. Even now, sitting atop his desk with his sneakers dangling over the edge, he appeared relaxed. David had agreed to wait for the child in the corridor.

"I'm so sorry about what I said before," said Oriana. "About you prying and all that. I was having a bad moment and I took it out on you."

"No worries, Mrs. Hapley," replied Walt. "At first, I felt hurt. But then I figured out you were upset about something else. It can happen to anyone."

"It can," echoed Oriana. "Can't it?"

Walt was such an insightful child, in some ways, wise beyond his years—and in others, so very naïve. Oriana refused to think about what would happen to him next—about where he was going, about what his future might hold. She would just do her part and attempt to move on. "I have something serious to discuss with you," she said.

"I'm not in trouble, am I?" he asked.

"Not exactly," she replied. "Do you remember that man who came to visit us today? Mr. David?"

And suddenly the boy knew. She could tell he knew by the way his expression tightened, the way his eyes abruptly lost their luster. He understood, and he despised her for being a part of it, for betraying his faith in her—after all the blossoms he'd brought her, the poppies, the hollyhocks, the gladiolas. Oriana reached for his arm on the walk to the limousine, but he viciously shook her off.

"You'll make a great teacher someday, Walt," she said, as the boy climbed into the black forbidding vehicle. She'd been instructed to avoid causing a scene, but she couldn't stop herself. "We'll have classrooms side by side," she cried. "Promise."

Oriana swore that she'd never forget the brave child who vanished behind those tinted windows without so much as a tear—although she knew not to discuss his absence with his classmates, not to draw attention to their loss. She did find herself thinking about him often, in those final months of her pregnancy, and then less. Soon enough, he'd be no different from the others: one of so many magical creatures who'd shared the tiny chairs of her classroom for a fleeting moment before moving on.

JURY OF MATRONS

———

My mother came from a family of relentless and intransigent women. One of her grandmothers—as Aunt Faye relished telling it—hatcheted saloons alongside Carrie Nation; the other operated the speakeasy where Joe Majczek and Ted Marcinkiewicz allegedly shot a Chicago traffic cop in 1932. ("You've probably seen the movie version," Aunt Faye crowed to friends. "*Call Northside 777*. June Havoc—you remember June Havoc, don't you?—has a bit part as my Granny Bess. Not credited, but still!") My mother's mother, Ida, fought alongside the Loyalists in Spain and later guided anti-Vichy partisans over the Pyrenees, albeit with limited success. So when my own mother deposited my bassinet in her aunt's parlor in Powick Bridge, a fruitless suburb of Hartford, Connecticut, and flew off to liberate Guatemala from *Yanquis*, she followed well-tread, if reckless, footsteps, and when she "disappeared" during the worst of that nation's "White Terror"—a named target of Colonel Arana's death brigades—the U.S. State Department offered Aunt Faye the diplomatic equivalent of a shrug. Fast forward fifteen years: that's a long about way of explaining how I, a perpetually flummoxed adolescent boy, ended up at my grandaunt's home, sharing a roof (and a cast-iron claw-foot bathtub) with three inscrutable women, when my mother's baby sister, Marcella, passed through en route from a halfway house in Springfield to the coast. "I'm going to save the Pregnant Pirette from the soldering iron, so help me," she announced to Aunt Faye. "And I'm taking Ginny's kid with me."

Marcella wore her tawny hair in cornrows tufted with cowry shells; her harem skirt flowed from a belt garnished with artificial daisies—but even in her thirties, our visitor looked too battle-worn for Hippiedom. (Try to picture Mrs. Khrushchev dressed as Bo Derek.) She dropped a carpet bag lacquered with political pins onto the front porch like a conquistador planting a flag.

"Like hell you are," replied my grandaunt, arms akimbo in the doorway.

I watched from the foyer. I was an animal carcass, pierced with a pair of bullet holes, at the mercy of two rival huntresses.

-⫷⫸-

When I'd first gone to live with Aunt Faye, she was alone in the house. She'd once had a husband, a fellow named Tate, but like most of the men in our family, he'd drifted from history into mist, leaving behind only his surname and not much else. (All I knew of my own father, Len Kuritsky, was that he'd asphyxiated on a chicken bone at a music festival in California several weeks after my birth.) At some point, long before I entered the scene, Aunt Faye had staffed the reference desk at the Powick Bridge Public Library, and, pushing seventy, she carried with her an atmosphere of dusty encyclopedias. We had lots of visitors in those days: a klatch of female relations whose precise perch on the family tree wasn't worth locating. Even Marcella had stayed overnight once but left in a huff before breakfast, incensed that Aunt Faye had stipulated a separate bed downstairs for her niece's boyfriend. Four years later, a widowed girlhood friend of my grandaunt—the aptly named Edie Coffin—moved permanently into the same chamber. (To this day, I don't know whether Aunt Faye and "Cousin" Edie were lovers, or had once been lovers, or were merely faithful late-life companions.) The third female in our estrogen-perfumed Cape Codder,

Cindy Jane, arrived only four months before Marcella. She was a genuine cousin—the sixteen-year-old, cashew-shaped, eggplant-hued spawn of two heroin junkies, one of them loosely descended from Granny Bess. Aunt Faye had again opened her doors to the family's jetsam.

So that's how the household stood at the outset of the battle royal. Marcella had just completed a ninety-nine-day stint in the Hampden County lockup for pepper-spraying a guard during protests against expanding an air force base, so she had more than three months of pent-up zeal to launch on behalf of her mission. It was a Saturday in July—a lazy, torrid afternoon—and although we'd been summarily banished to the yard seconds after Marcella's arrival, both Cindy Jane and I eavesdropped from below the kitchen window. The heavy scent of "Cousin" Edie's heliotrope and sweet alyssum cloyed our nostrils.

"I'm sorry, dear," said Aunt Faye. "I am glad to see you're well—and you're always welcome in this house, provided you abide by the house rules. That being said, I cannot have you showing up here like the Pied Piper of Hamelin and leading that boy into trouble."

"Nobody is leading anyone into trouble, Faye. I'm teaching the boy the value of direct action, of bearing witness. Doesn't it bother you the slightest bit that they're going to guillotine the Pregnant Pirette on a whim?"

"I doubt they're doing anything on a whim," replied Aunt Faye. "In the first place, you act like it's a human being they're harming. They're dismantling a statue, for heaven's sake. A rusted old iron statue that nobody—at least nobody other than you—gives a slap about. It's not as though you're trying to save an ancient redwood or some natural wonder—"

"It's a feminist icon—"

"Do let me finish, dear. As far as I'm concerned, I think it's a wise choice they're making, razing all those blighted motels and creating a preserve. And so too, I might add, does every progressive thinker and environmental scientist in this state."

"Not every—"

"*Almost* every one. Your problem, Marcella, if you'd like my unsolicited

opinion—and even if you don't—is that you're always looking for causes."
Once Aunt Faye dipped into her speak-in-full-paragraphs mode, there was
no turning back. "I'm not saying the world is a perfectly just place, but it's
not the gulag either. Even without a revolution, we have running water, and
three solid meals a day, and the right to vote and to speak our minds and to
make pests of ourselves in public places. Maybe you could try being thankful
for a change. In any event, the bottom line is that you're welcome to drive
down to East Sedley and make a nuisance of yourself all you'd like—get
yourself arrested again, if you have your heart set on it—but I have custody
of that boy, and he's not getting wrapped up in your shenanigans."

Marcella responded with a sigh—almost a groan—that seemingly
contained all of the frustrations of Woodstock and Selma and Kent State
drawn into one breath. "What planet do you live on, Faye Tate? Do you
really believe all that Norman Rockwell shit about the right to speak your
mind? Jesus-fucking-Christ! That statue is a landmark. A piece of my
childhood. She was practically my best friend. Have you forgotten how
I'd stuff pillows under my nightgown and go down to the beach at night
to help her defend our motel from marauders while you and that bald lady
friend of yours got sloshed on cocktails?"

"Betty Miniver was not bald; she had alopecia. Nor did either of us ever
'get sloshed,' as you call it. That's simply *not* what your childhood was like."

"Maybe you weren't sober enough to remember."

"Enough, young lady," counseled Aunt Faye. "Now put your bag in
the upstairs guest room and I'll make you some cucumber sandwiches to
tide you over until supper."

Cindy Jane poked my flank and whispered, "Crazy how they're fighting over you, isn't it?"

That was before I'd decided whether I found Cindy Jane attractive
enough to kiss. "I guess," I agreed—not too committal.

"You know what? I bet Marcella isn't your aunt at all," said Cindy Jane,
her warm breath only inches from my neck. "I bet she's really your mother."

-᪥᪥᪥◆᪥᪥᪥-

Aunt Faye called us into the house again before Cindy Jane could elaborate, so it wasn't until nearly midnight that she pressed her point. We'd tiptoed downstairs—lungs held past Edie's bedroom—and then through the cellar door into the yard, where the previous owner had wedged a tree house into a colossal black walnut. Nearly every weekend night since school let out, the pair of us had been meeting up atop those pinewood boards, his and hers milk-crate stools roosted a thirty-foot climb above the lawn by rope ladder, squandering time and whetting lust. The truth was that I couldn't imagine kissing Cindy Jane without my eyes clenched shut—she had caterpillar brows and a knob of baby fat under her chin—but I weighed a scrawny one-hundred-thirty-pounds in my tennis shoes, and other girls hadn't lined up outside my door. (The only girl I'd ever asked out, strawberry-haired Angie Swenson, responded to me much as the State Department had responded to Aunt Faye.) So I faced the teenage loser's ultimate dilemma: pine after girls like Angie until fate shifted the tides or make out with my cousin. *A bush in hand or a bird in flight*, as they say. I reassured myself that Cindy Jane and I shared only a fraction of DNA.

Don't get me wrong: Cindy Jane hadn't exactly been offering up her lips for the taking. Yet I sensed that if I mustered the courage to ask, I might receive what I wasn't sure I actually wanted. In the meantime, while the more popular 98 percent of Dean Acheson High School's tenth-grade class bonded at sleep-away camps in the Berkshires—a concept as alien to spendthrift Aunt Faye as store-pitted cherries—we engaged in a lopsided flirtation, a pas de deux rendered all the more alluring by its concealment. (I must have been in my late thirties—as old as Marcella was then—when I realized that Aunt Faye had known of our nocturnal trysts all along, although I'm still unsure whether she was hoping to encourage a "romance" between us.) Cindy Jane had pinched a coconut-scented candle while babysitting for a neighbor and had smuggled it into the tree house. The flame danced off her pajama top, illuminating her bounteous breasts.

"C'mon, Pete," insisted Cindy Jane. "You can't really think it's a coincidence they're both tugging on you like a wishbone. Did you notice how

Marcella didn't mention your so-called mother at all in her story about the pirate statue? Not even once."

"Why would she?"

"Because your mother must have been there with her and Faye in East Sedley? And if she wasn't, *where was she* while Faye and her bald gal pal were getting sloppy?"

"I don't know," I said. "Someplace else."

"And don't you think it's weird that they don't have any of your mother's stuff around this house? Not even newspaper clippings? They have a basement full of Marcella's junk—Marcella's punching bag and Marcella's talking Barbie and Marcella's Go-Go the Burro—a whole damn shrine to one niece—and nothing of your mom's except a couple of snapshots that could be anybody." Cindy Jane adjusted the candle to shield it from the draft. "I mean there are ten times more photos of my own deadbeat mama in Faye's albums than of your mother, and my mama is like a billionth cousin two zillion times removed."

"Mom only lived here a few years," I argued anemically. "She was already a teenager when grandma died. *Marcella grew up here.*"

"Whatever." Cindy Jane folded her arms across her chest. "I'm telling you that woman they claim is your mother is a cover story. Maybe she was a family friend—or a distant relative of some sort—if she even existed at all. Marcella is your mother."

I suppose my orphan's ears were primed for my cousin's charge, because I found my resistance waning. "I don't get it. Why would they lie?"

"Who knows? Marcella probably couldn't manage both a baby and a revolution, so she abandoned you here, and in return for raising you, Faye made her promise not to tell." Cindy Jane inched her milk crate closer to mine. "Women used to do that all the time, grandmothers pretending they were mothers, and mother pretending they were sisters. . . . Don't be so fucking naïve, Pete. That's how the world works."

You're thinking her theory sounds like the plot of a Dickens novel— and a bad one at that—that no marginally sane teenage boy could ever embrace such a tale. All I can say is that it's different if you've grown up without a mother, if you sobbed yourself to sleep countless nights over a woman you don't even remember, if you've spent your whole childhood fantasizing that a two-line cable from Guatemala was sent in error. "Marcella is too young to be my mother anyway," I said, serving up one last defensive salvo.

"Bullshit. How old is she? Thirty-eight? Thirty-nine? You do the math," said Cindy Jane. "I was certainly old enough to have a baby at thirteen."

This reference to her own sexual maturity galvanized the atmosphere in the tree house. Cindy Jane glanced down at her knees, her chubby knees that I suddenly imagined spreading with my palms. I felt the tips of my ears ablaze.

"Do you really think she's my mother?" I asked—mostly to fill the shadows with words. "How can you be so sure?"

Cindy Jane looked pensive as though victim to an internal struggle. Outside, raccoons scampered in the undergrowth. The electric lantern on Mrs. Sewell's porch cast a hostile beam into "Cousin" Edie's strawberry patch.

"I'll make you a deal. Tell me I'm pretty and I'll tell you a secret."

This was not the first time, nor the last, that Cindy Jane bartered for compliments.

I tried to meet her demand without lying, but that seemed an insurmountable challenge. "You're my cousin," I said. "Of course, I think you're pretty."

Cindy Jane weighed my answer—deciding whether to be flattered or insulted. "Okay, thank you," she finally said. "So I'm going to share this with you, but swear you won't tell a soul."

I swore—right hand raised like in a courtroom: "May the Red Sox finish dead last for a hundred seasons if I tell." A barn owl shrieked in the darkness, mocking my oath.

"You'd better not say a word," my cousin warned. She leaned forward, her lips only inches from mine. I smelled the cinnamon gum on her breath. "When I was two or three years old, Marcella stayed with my parents in

Berkeley. I can't recall much about the visit, but I do remember one thing for certain—she wasn't alone. She came with a baby."

Cindy Jane curled her lips into a tooth-crammed grin. Never have I seen another human being appear as self-assured as she did following her revelation.

"That doesn't prove anything," I said. My body, quavering violently, cried otherwise.

⋘◆⋙

The next morning, while Aunt Faye griddled waffles, Marcella corralled me into the parlor and shared the saga of the Pregnant Pirette, preparing me for the Tuesday morning rally I'd been barred from attending. "You'd be surprised how many female buccaneers there were in their heyday. . . . Anne Bonny, Mary Read, Rachel Wall," she explained. "Jacquotte Delahaye, who faked her own death." While she spoke, I scrutinized her face, trying to read a likeness to my own drab features. I smoldered to ask her pointblank: *Are you my mother?* But I didn't dare—suspecting she would lie, but also fearful of upsetting my own fantasy. Soon "Cousin" Edie settled into the armchair opposite the bay windows, as she did every morning, stripping us of any vestige of privacy.

Marcella didn't even acknowledge Edie's arrival. She asked me: "Do you know what happened to female buccaneers when they were caught?"

I delved deep into my piratical knowledge, most of it gleaned from *Treasure Island* and *Peter Pan*. "They walked the plank?"

"Close. They hanged," answered Marcella. "Unless they were pregnant."

Edie flashed a frown in our direction but said nothing. In the foyer, the grandfather clock knelled a joyless eight o'clock.

"If the baby inside them was old enough for people to feel—a stage called quickening—then they were spared the gallows until they gave birth. And often, by then, they'd managed to escape or obtain a pardon."

I studied Marcella's cheeks, her jawline. We shared a chiseled nose—distinctive on her, I suppose, but too large for my narrow skull. I resembled her more, I decided, than the soft-featured brunette who appeared sporadically in Aunt Faye's albums. Edie lit a cigarette—Virginia Slims—filling the parlor with the heady cologne of tobacco.

"So they had groups of women whose job it was to decide which pirettes were actually pregnant and which were lying," continued Marcella. "These were called juries of matrons."

I sensed a lethal presence in the room and looked up to find Aunt Faye, armored in plaid apron and oven mitts, scowling at her niece. "It's time you stopped filling that boy's mind with claptrap," she declared. "What does he care about lady pirates?"

"I'm teaching him about the world," retorted Marcella. She turned to me and added, "A pirette takes what she wants. Unlike many modern women."

That was too much for my grandaunt. "The world can fix its own problems. You'd be better off figuring out what you're going to do with your life, don't you think?"

"I'm already doing something with my life."

They stood facing each other—the woman who'd raised me and the woman who might have birthed me—like eighteenth-century musketeers in hostile formation. Cindy Jane had stationed herself at the top of the stairs to survey the battlefield.

"I'd like to have a word with you in private, Marcella," said Aunt Faye.

Marcella refused to make eye contact. "If you have anything you want to say to me, you can say it right here. I don't have any secrets."

"Well I have secrets. Plenty of them. And while you're eating my food and sleeping on my bedding, young lady, you'll just as soon give me a moment of your time."

The innuendo about secrets was not lost on me. Cindy Jane beamed knowingly.

Marcella didn't say a word, but she slowly—at the pace of a molasses-dipped tortoise—climbed off the sofa and trailed Aunt Faye into the kitchen. The heavy oak door swung shut behind them, muffling the ensuing row. "I have an idea," suggested Edie Coffin. "Why don't we three play a round of pinochle?" Any hope of overhearing the conflagration in the next room was soon drowned out in the widow's squeals of "Aces abound!" and "Nine of trump!" Cindy Jane and I conducted an entire conversation with our facial muscles.

Secretly, I hoped for a revelation—like King Solomon offering to split the baby in half—that would expose my mother's true identity. Instead, a subdued Marcella, with streaks of eyeliner trailing below her orbits, eventually pushed open the swinging door.

"We've reached a compromise, Peter," she announced. "Faye has agreed to let me take you to see the Pregnant Pirette tomorrow. But then I'll bring you back here and I'll go to Tuesday's demonstration alone."

Aunt Faye emerged from the kitchen. "And the other half?"

Marcella's voice tensed up. "I've agreed that she can come with us."

--«««•»»»-

One advantage of having Aunt Faye accompany us was that we could drive her Oldsmobile directly to the coast, rather than calling a cab to take us to the bus station. Around ten o'clock the next morning, we piled into that oversized vehicle—my grandaunt behind the wheel, a cooler of turkey sandwiches and fruit punch in the trunk—and headed toward Long Island Sound. Edie stayed home to look after the house. "What do I want with pirates?" she asked. (I'm honestly not sure if Edie Coffin stepped foot from that house even once between the day she moved in and Aunt Faye's funeral; my grandaunt's will left her the place, in trust, and when I visited Edie in her final years, the widow's sole goal was surviving until the mint issued the last of its fifty-state commemorative quarters, which she collected like relics.) Cindy Jane also had to remain in Powder Bridge, much to her consternation, because Aunt Faye declared, "I can't be responsible for looking after two wild children at once." That Marcella was so desperate to show me the statue, but obviously less vested in my cousin, struck us both as telling.

A skilled driver could reach East Sedley from Powick Bridge in under ninety minutes. Aunt Faye managed the trip in slightly over three hours. She refused to leave the right lane, even when we found ourselves behind a trailer hauling cement pylons, and she stopped at every public restroom in Southern Connecticut. While we drove, Marcella furthered my education in the field of female piracy. I entered a panorama of cross-dressing bandits and swashbuckling maidens who fed English admirals to sharks. Marcella possessed a gift for elucidating the underlying political implications of the most innocuous-seeming yarns. "Often a considerable time passed between when these women were apprehended and when they arrived on shore to plead the belly," she said. "So a class of professional 'baby getters' seized the opportunity. These were able seamen in the Royal Navy who'd knock up accused women for a small share of their pirate's loot—or even for amusement." I found myself both fascinated by this revelation and mortified that Marcella had shared it.

"Don't you think that's enough?" asked Aunt Faye.

"I don't see the point of sheltering him," snapped Marcella. "He should have some idea of what women have gone through to get where we are."

"Not all women were pirates," said Aunt Faye.

I sensed the two of them were engaged in a complex emotional ballet, employing military stratagems of Napoleonic proportions, tactics that made the pas de deux between me and Cindy Jane look like an amateur checkers match. In some ways, I felt irrelevant to the entire struggle—a pawn, an afterthought—and then the notion hit me that maybe I was an afterthought. If Marcella could be my mother, why couldn't Faye be her mother? Suddenly, all of the enigmatic twists of my childhood yielded their mystery.

"Ginny would want him to know," said Marcella.

"I don't doubt she would," answered Aunt Faye. "But Ginny's not here."

My grandaunt's words sounded more like a warning than a statement.

After that, we drove in silence until we reach the coast.

East Sedley did not live up to my hopes. The resort had once been a summer retreat for upper-middle-class New Englanders—Waspy physicians and insurance executives who wished to avoid the nouveau riche Jews, like my father, who'd "taken over" Watch Hill and Nantucket. By the early 1980s, the town center consisted of a shuttered movie house, a flyblown post office, and a post-and-beam library open three mornings each week. Of the two dozen motels that had lined the beach from the marina to the Rhode Island border, only one—the Captain's Deck—remained operational. All of the others, including the Vengeful Scrod, where my family had summered, and the adjacent Jolly Roger, whose beachfront harbored the Pregnant Pirette, had been commandeered by the state in eminent domain proceedings.

Aunt Faye eased the Oldsmobile onto the gravel lot opposite the remnants of the Jolly Roger. The letters V CAN Y welcomed us in unlit neon. Beyond a chain-link fence rose the steel shoulders and bulging metallic tummy of the Pirette. Rigging cascaded down her back in a knotty mane. A corrugated patch covered her left eye. The fabric shielding her breasts had long since peeled away, exposing two jagged-edged cones. Nearby, a Caterpillar bulldozer lurked in a pit of sand, temporarily deserted, awaiting its turn at the Pirette.

Marcella hiked through the litter-strewn no-man's-land between the road and the construction site, kicking aside the orange traffic cones and yellow police tape that walled off the public from the padlocked gate. She cupped the lock for a moment, then let it fall against the meshwork with a clatter. Overhead, terns and herring gulls circled for prey.

I let the sea breeze fill my lungs with salt.

"Satisfied?" asked Aunt Faye.

Marcella glowered at her. "Very."

The pair of them certainly interacted like mother and daughter.

-≪≪◆≫≫-

Our outing sounded all the more uneventful when I shared the details with Cindy Jane later that evening while Aunt Faye and Cousin Edie prepared supper. I described Marcella's failed effort to scale the fence, her dust up with my grandaunt, the numerous times she declared that my mother would have wanted me to see the Pirette. I related our brief detour to a specialty knitting shop in Branford, east of New Haven, where Aunt Faye picked up a ball of Merino yarn for her next afghan. "If I'm gallivanting halfway to the moon," she said, "I might as well make good use of the gasoline." I complained to Cindy Jane of the gargantuan mosquitos that guarded the statue. I pointedly omitted my theory of multiple generations of family deception. Once we'd been summoned to the dining room, nobody made mention of the excursion at all.

A truce had settled over the household. Aunt Faye acknowledged that there "was no harm" in my seeing a historic landmark like the Pirette, which she conceded "could be considered a feminist icon" from a certain perspective. Marcella made a point of including Edie Coffin in the conversation, asking after her tea roses and stamp collection. Cindy Jane scrawled the words, *Are you my mother?* on her napkin and slid it onto my lap. By the time Aunt Faye served the apple cobbler, we were actually laughing like a family.

That night, I dreamed that I'd accompanied my mom to the Guatemalan Highlands. We trekked from village to village, organizing the K'iche' people for revolt. Somehow, I was both an infant and a teenager at the same time, so when the death squads finally caught up with our band—while my mother was away, spying on a nearby quarry—I pretended to be a sleeping child and managed to survive the ensuing massacre. I balled up my limbs, frozen, until my mom returned to the bloodbath and shook me awake. She kept shaking me, so I opened my eyes, and there stood Marcella, in my dimly lit bedroom, a finger over her lips. At her urging, I dressed rapidly and followed her downstairs. The grandfather clock in the foyer read four a.m.

Marcella didn't have to tell me where we were going. As soon as I saw her retrieve the keys to Aunt Faye's Oldsmobile from the wall hook in the kitchen, I understood we were headed back to the coast to help rescue the Pregnant Pirette.

"It's raining," whispered Marcella. "Do you have a jacket?"

Her words sounded maternal, not auntly. No teenage boy has ever been so thrilled to be told to bundle up. I retrieved my windbreaker from the hall closet.

Route 89 extended clear as an airport runway in the predawn. Steam rose off the asphalt. We crossed the Powick River and gusts rattled the chassis of the Oldsmobile. Marcella drove at literally twice the speed of my grandaunt, peeling turns and passing busses on the right. She'd flipped the radio to a folk station and the car filled with the sounds of The Original Caste commemorating "One Tin Soldier." I dozed to the rhythms of the highway. When I woke again, we were already on the outskirts of East Sedley.

"Good, you're up," said Marcella.

She stopped for carryout coffee at a ramshackle café.

"How do you like yours?" she asked.

I didn't. But I hoped to sound mature. "Black," I said.

She poured cream and sugar into her own cup.

"If you're not part of the solution, you're part of the problem," said Marcella. It wasn't until my second semester at Yale that I realized the quote was Eldridge Cleaver's, not hers. "Faye is part of the problem. Ginny would want you to be part of the solution."

"Aunt Faye tries her best," I said protectively.

"I know that," agreed Marcella. "But sometimes that's not good enough."

We climbed back into the car and soon pulled up in front of the Jolly Roger. Several of the demonstrators had already arrived, including an elderly woman with a bolt cutter. Also on hand was a morbidly obese man in his sixties, the brother of the sculptor. Next a lesbian couple arrived, then an unkempt family of six. By daybreak, other protestors—mostly women, mostly over forty—had arrived with placards that read "Saws off my Belly," the rallying cry of the Pirette-preservation movement, but also "Close Yankee Power" and "Save Narragansett Bay" and "Reagan = War Criminal." One activist distributed flyers demanding immediate pardons

for Eddie Conway and Leonard Peltier. Another, whose outfit reminded
me of Danny Kaye channeling a court jester, connected the statue's fate
to the plight of Palestine and Tibet. At full deployment, the campaigners
numbered about thirty.

I hoped that Marcella might introduce me as her son, but she didn't.
"This is my nephew, Peter," she said—and each time she said 'nephew,' I
felt disowned. My nose and chin grew raw from the spray-brined air.

The construction crew arrived around nine o'clock—a half dozen
sun-scarred men in coveralls and hard hats. I'd anticipated warfare, but
the demolition team appeared largely indifferent to the disruption. They
got paid, it seemed, either way. Only their foreman expressed any displea-
sure. "This here is private property," he shouted over the protesters' off-key
chorus of "We Shall Overcome." "I'm going to have to call the authorities.
You're leaving me no choice."

He returned ten minutes later and said, "Please, be reasonable. Look,
people, you're going to get yourselves in trouble. I'm warning you."

Our ragtag band sang louder. Marcella squeezed my forearm.

"Your mother would be so proud," she said. "We're going to win."

I trusted her. "Do you really think so?"

"Of course, I do. The momentum is on our side. And so is justice.
Once they realize what the Pregnant Pirette means to us—as women, as
human beings—they'll back down."

We were still singing when the squad cars arrived. New London
Country Sheriff. Two officers in each. They approached us, communicat-
ing in their own dialect of nods and gestures, and I feared they might
break out stun grenades or teargas canisters, like the military police had
done when Marcella refused to leave the air force base. To my amazement,
one of them asked—in a voice firm, but not unkind—"Are you Peter
Kuritsky?"

I honestly don't remember what I answered, or even if I answered at
all. I have only the vaguest recollection of climbing into the rear seat of
the cruiser, followed by Marcella, who apologized to the other demonstrators before departing. "A misunderstanding," she pleaded. "We'll be

back as soon as we sort this all out." Today, I imagine she'd have been arrested for kidnapping, but those were laxer times. All the authorities wanted to do—and the senior officer explained this patiently, between Marcella's threats—was to return us both to Powick Bridge, where Aunt Faye waited at the stationhouse. "If it's a misunderstanding, ma'am," he said, "the local police will sort it out for you." Yet when the vehicle's door shut behind us, the clink sounded like the closing of a prison cell. East Sedley retreated into the past.

I watched the cops in the front of the cruiser, but they were ignoring us. My window of opportunity was closing: If I wanted to know the truth, this was the moment. I counted to ten and played all my cards. "Marcella, can I ask you a question about the time you visited Cindy Jane's parents in Berkeley?"

Marcella turned toward me. Surprised. Puzzled. "What?"

I didn't need to hear anything more. I already knew the truth—I could see it in her confusion—and I fought back my tears. Not only was Marcella not my mother and Aunt Faye not my grandmother, but the Pregnant Pirette would soon land in a scrapheap, and no lifetime of tides would unite me with Angie Swenson, and no matter how many times you watch *Northside 777*, you won't see the actress June Havoc in an uncredited role as my great-grandmother, because she doesn't appear in the film. Not at all.

-⫷⫷◆⫸⫸-

"She really called the police?" said Cindy Jane. "Wow! That's crazy."

Although it was a weeknight, we'd rendezvoused in the tree house. Marcella was long gone and another eight years would elapse before we heard from her again: a get well card that arrived—too late—after Aunt Faye's second stroke. My grandaunt had offered to pay for a taxi, but Marcella insisted on hitchhiking to the train station. Outside, a cold front had left a damp nip in the summer air. Fireflies pulsed in the yard below; a whip-poor-will wailed. My wrists and ankles itched from where I'd been nibbled by mosquitos.

"Did you get to ask her whether she's really your mother?" asked Cindy Jane.

"Why bother?" I replied. "She'd lie either way."

I let Cindy Jane absorb my indifference. She looked wounded.

"Let's talk about something else," I suggested, seizing the advantage.

Cindy Jane's voice turned coy. "Like what?"

My eyes casually raked over her flannel-covered legs, her cleavage.

"I have an idea," I said. "Let's not talk at all. Let's kiss."

My audacity surprised even me—as though I was the first teenager ever to ask for a kiss.

"I'll make you a deal," offered Cindy Jane, as though she'd had the words stockpiled. "If you tell me you love me and you'll be my boyfriend, I'll kiss you."

So I told her the lies she asked for—and then I leaned into her with my eyes clenched, ready to start making my way in the world.

GABLE'S WHISKERS

-≪≪◆≫≫-

In Aldama's nightmare, Robustelli severed an ear.

They had the barbershop to themselves that afternoon—Bernal's chair stood vacant between them—and customers crowded the benches along the window. It must have been a Saturday, because Aldama recognized several weekend regulars: Steinhoff, the florist from across the street; the twelve-year-old triplets whose mother insisted on distinct haircuts; Dr. Sucram, who gave him a case of his private-label Riesling every Christmas. More patrons waited on the sidewalk. Every man in Hager Heights, it seemed, had chosen that afternoon for a trim. Aldama focused on the client in front of him, paying little attention to his elderly colleague, but at some point he glanced toward the old man's corner, and to his horror, discovered the Italian running a straight razor along the lathered sideburns of the state health inspector. Robustelli's arm shook—not a mild tremor, but the wild quake of infirmity. Aldama pleaded with the old man to be careful—the state inspector might shutter the place on a whim—but Robustelli merely laughed and kept shaving. "*Finito*," he finally declared. "*Perfetto.*" He held a mirror behind the state inspector's head, displaying the man's reflection for approval, revealing the bloody socket where his ear had once been. And then, suddenly, Aldama was awake, and he was still renting a chair to Robustelli.

"Jesus, Adolfo, you're sweating," cried his wife. "Do you have a fever?" He shook her hand off his forehead. The beams of the streetlight sliced through the blinds, casting horizontal bars across the duvet.

"Not a fever. A bad dream."

The barber recognized that sharing his nightmare with Nilda could only add to his worries—his wife had a knack for using his own dreams against him—but after thirty-eight years of marriage, he also knew he'd end up telling her eventually. Besides, this time she'd be right. He *did* need to speak to Robustelli. Otherwise, eventually, the Italian would end up severing an ear. But he'd been meaning to act since March, when the poor fellow shattered the bottle of sterilizer. Now it was June. All he'd actually done over the course of two months was to increase his E & O insurance.

"It's the old man, isn't it?" demanded Nilda.

Aldama said nothing. She'd been on his case for weeks.

"Do you want me to speak to him?" she asked—and he had little doubt that she'd actually follow through on the threat, if he'd allowed her. That was the difference between them, but also the bond that held them together while all four of his brothers, even Ramón back in Havana, were now divorced. He was a dreamer trapped in the body of a suburban barber. Nilda didn't have an ounce of sentiment in her veins.

"I'll do it. I told you I'll do it."

"When? After he slits somebody's throat?"

Nilda had flipped on her bedside lamp. That meant she wanted to hash the matter out; he wanted to return to sleep.

"Okay, Adolfo. He's an old man. You don't want to throw him out on the street. I understand that," said Nilda. "But what about me? What about Gloria? How do you plan on telling your own daughter that you can't pay for her wedding because all of her papa's money went to fight a lawsuit?"

"I'm not disagreeing with you," said Aldama.

"Okay, he's an old man. The world is full of old men." Nilda continued. "And old dogs too. And orphaned children."

"Tomorrow," pledged Aldama. "Now let's get some sleep."

But Nilda wasn't quite done. "What does Bernal say?" she asked.

Bernal was Nilda's cousin, her aunt's grandson. He'd been renting the middle chair from Aldama for almost two decades, and while the young man worked hard and was perfectly responsible in every way, his good cheer grated on the barber's nerves.

"He agrees with you."

"See. Even Bernal agrees with me," said Nilda. "Do you know why? Because he has his priorities straight. What's going to happen to Bernal's baby when that old man lops somebody's ear off?"

Aldama closed his eyes, pretending to sleep. He knew that he wasn't fooling his wife, of course, but she'd already had her say—at least, for the moment—and after feeling his forehead a final time, she switched off the bedside lamp.

-≪◆≫-

Robustelli had appeared one evening the previous summer. He'd knocked on the plate glass after hours, while Aldama was sweeping the linoleum, and initially the barber had mistaken him for a customer and shaken his head. Only when the old man's fingers mimicked a scissors did Aldama understand that he'd come about the open chair. That had been about a month after Enriqué, who'd shared the workspace with Aldama for nearly three decades, had retired to Orlando. In the interim, he'd interviewed an overweight black woman named Birdie and an effeminate guy in his twenties, fresh out of training, who described himself as a "stylist." Neither seemed promising. Aldama liked both applicants well enough personally— more than he liked his wife's cousin, in truth—but they didn't fit the Old World ambience that attracted his clientele. Besides, Bernal refused to work alongside a homosexual. Yet now the chair had sat empty for almost five weeks, earning nothing, like cash buried under a rock.

"I couldn't find the darn place," said the newcomer, as though his arrival had been expected. "They said ten minutes' walk from the train. It's more like thirty."

The old man—he looked to be beyond seventy, even pushing eighty—sported a bowtie, a vest and a Homburg hat; he'd draped his jacket over his arm as a concession to the August heat. In his opposite hand, he carried a well-worn Gladstone bag, which he set down with a thud. "I hear you're looking for a barber," said Robustelli. "And I'm a barber." He extended his hand. "Vittorio Robustelli, at your service."

Aldama introduced himself. The Italian's manner seemed so dramatic, so contrived, that for a moment, he feared that he was being mocked. "Do you have an up-to-date New York state license? References?"

"A license, yes," answered Robustelli. "I've been cutting hair longer than most men have been alive. I've had my brushes with history, too. When I owned my place across from the United Nations, I shaved Eisenhower and Khrushchev during the same week."

"And references?" asked Aldama.

"You don't believe me? No matter. It is true," said Robustelli. He stooped over his bag and removed his framed license; a jagged crack bisected the glass shield. "When Clark Gable was asked to cut off his mustache for *Mutiny on the Bounty*, who clipped his whiskers? Robustelli, that's who." The old man set his license on the countertop alongside Bernal's; as a young man, Aldama noted, he'd been strikingly handsome.

"Gable brought along a felt-lined jewelry box from Tiffany's," said Robustelli, dusting off his chair with a rag of his own supply. "He had me set his whiskers in the box like I was laying an infant in a casket. *That*, I will never forget."

"References?" repeated Aldama.

The Italian said nothing, his eyes focused on his bag.

"I owned my own shop," he said. "How should I get references?"

Aldama knew he ought to make further inquiries: How had Robustelli learned of the open chair? What had become of his shop? Had he ever injured a client? That's what Nilda would have done. Or Bernal. But he liked what he saw of the old man—his energy, his formal dress—and he sensed, deep down, that he was better off not knowing what had led Robustelli to his door.

Aldama seated himself in the spare chair and tucked his sunglasses into his breast pocket. "All right. Let's see what you've got."

Robustelli grinned. He reached into his bag, which contained a vast assortment of sprays and powders, and removed a pair of shears. Soon he was pruning Aldama's skull while relating the details of his tonsorial encounter with Sir Anthony Eden. The man snipped more air than hair—and he wasn't going to win any prizes for speed. Yet the final product appeared competent enough. "We take customers in order," said Aldama. "No reservations. I'm not running a motel." And that was that.

-⫷⫸-

At first, the Italian proved a good fit for the shop. He worked long hours, never complained and kept his workspace immaculate. Even Bernal, who'd resented not being consulted on Aldama's decision, conceded that the newcomer added "a certain charm" to the establishment. Most important, the customers like Robustelli. The old man knew a story for every occasion, a tale that always involved a bygone celebrity or statesman and a heroic barber by the name of Robustelli.

"One time, Groucho Marx's regular barber came down with tuberculosis, and he called for a stand-in," began a typical morning. Or, "When Bob Denver needed his goatee shaped for the Dobie Gillis show." Many of the stories repeated themselves too. By the end of the summer, Aldama could recount the Italian's meetings with Clark Gable and Lucky Luciano as though he'd witnessed them firsthand. Some of these encounters seemed more plausible than others—and a few, downright unlikely. When a teenage customer pointed out that *Mutiny on the Bounty* had been filmed in the mid-1930s, which meant that Robustelli was either over ninety-five or lying, the barber laughed and said, "Scoff, young man. Go ahead. See if Robustelli cares." He shook his head, as though disappointed in the youth. "I know the truth and that is what matters."

Aldama didn't care whose hair the Italian had cut or when—any more than he gave a damn about Bernal claiming to have a college degree, or

Gloria insisting that their ancestors had been Spanish nobility. Everybody had white lies they told themselves to get through the day, and if some people shared these minor falsehoods with others, what harm was done? Clearly, the Italian relished cutting hair, which was more than could be said for a lot of men in their trade. With his daughter getting married and his mother-in-law in the hospital, Robustelli's embellishments were the least of Aldama's concerns.

The trouble arose when Robustelli started to shake. At first, Aldama hadn't noticed anything amiss, so it was difficult to pinpoint the precise moment when the old man's grip grew unsteady—if such a precise moment had even existed. All the barber knew for certain was that one March afternoon Robustelli had lost his hold on a thirty-two-ounce bottle of sterilizer, splattering a balding dentist with glass shards and alcohol. The dentist, Dr. Kimball, had shown considerable understanding; he'd refused to send them his dry-cleaning bill and even over-tipped on his haircut. But ever since that incident, Aldama had become keenly aware of his colleague's worsening tremor.

"You should get that checked out," he urged Robustelli.

The Italian shrugged. "It's nothing. Hardly a twitch."

Eight weeks later, the "twitch" looked more like an earthquake or an epileptic fit, and customers had started to avoid the Italian's chair. When Aldama arrived at the shop, on the morning following his nightmare, three patrons were already waiting for service, while Bernal tended to a fourth. The Italian perched in his own chair, unwanted, reading the *Daily News* and wearing a stoic expression. His tremor rendered even turning the pages of the newspaper a time-consuming struggle.

Aldama tended to the men in line. Around ten o'clock, one of the managers from the vegan café around the corner came in—obviously in a hurry—and he let Robustelli run the electric razor over his scalp. An hour later, a scruffy college student asked to have his locks pared "to chin level" for a job interview. Every time the Italian raised his clippers above the level of the kid's chin, Aldama feared the youth might lose an eye. Eventually, when the line was down to one customer, a regular of Bernal's,

Aldama turned to the old man and suggested, "Let's grab some food, you and me."

"What if it gets busy again?" asked Robustelli.

"Bernal can handle it. Can't you, Bernal?"

Aldama threw his wife's cousin a pointed look. Bernal had already spoken to him twice about the old man's shakes. "Bring me back a regular coffee," said Bernal.

The Italian busied himself adjusting bottles on his work shelf.

"Let's get going," said Aldama. "Before the lunch crowd."

"Not today," pleaded Robustelli. "I don't have my wallet."

"On me," said Aldama. "I insist."

So the old man accompanied him to the boxcar diner that shared a shopping plaza with Steinhoff's Blossoms and Laurendale Tile & Marble. At the center of the pavilion stood the bare showroom that had until recently served an upscale furniture importer named Borrelli's. Before that, the site had housed a carpet dealer—and earlier, back in the 1980s, a video game arcade. According to one longtime barbershop customer, a retired accountant who'd lived in Hager Heights since the 1940s, a live poultry market had occupied the location during his childhood. An egg candling facility had once operated on the spot where Aldama's barbershop now stood.

In the diner—a musty, low-slung firetrap—they settled down at a booth beside the door. As soon as they'd ordered, Robustelli launched into a story about a chophouse owner in Midtown Manhattan who used to trade haircuts for steaks. Aldama toyed with his cutlery and let the old man talk. Eventually, when their meals arrived, Robustelli paused long enough to taste-check his soup for salt, creating the opening that Aldama both sought and dreaded.

"I'm worried about you, Vittorio," he said.

"That makes one of us. What is there to worry about?"

Aldama drew a deep breath and thought of his wife. "That shaking of yours," he said. "I'm sorry, but you have to see a doctor. You could hurt somebody."

The Italian didn't make eye contact. He added more salt to his soup.

"What's the big deal about going to a doctor? Maybe he could help you," pressed Aldama. "If it's about the cost, I can even contribute something."

Robustelli tucked a paper napkin into his collar.

"I've been to a doctor. A specialist in neurology. It cannot be fixed."

"Are you sure? Maybe a second opinion?"

Robustelli struggled to lift his soup spoon to his lips, but the tremor got in his way. After several attempts, which soaked the napkin, he pushed the bowl to the center of the table. Then he looked up into Aldama's eyes, and for the first since they'd met, Aldama sensed that the man across from him was not putting on a show.

"When my wife became ill, we went to a fancy doctor on Park Avenue for a second opinion," said Robustelli. "And then a third. And a fourth. But none of that changed anything. Vera's heart was still *malato*. Kaput." The Italian sighed. "In any event, I *did* obtain a second opinion. Last month." He shook his head.

"I can't let you hurt someone," said Aldama. "You have to understand."

The Italian grimaced. "I have been cutting hair for more than half a century. When I lost my lease, I told myself: Robustelli, you still have your trade. As long as you have a trade, you can do anything. . . . But now. . . . " The old man removed the napkin from his shirt collar and set it on the tabletop. "How will I support myself? Tell me that, if you're so worried about Vittorio Robustelli. How will I earn my bread?"

"You must have family," said Aldama. "What about Social Security?"

Robustelli frowned. "I have nothing," he said. "But you will do what *you* have to do and I will do what *I* have to do. So there we have it. I thank you for lunch."

When they returned to the shop, Robustelli invited the next waiting customer into his chair. Bernal glowered at Aldama. "If you'll lock up for me, Bernal," said Aldama, removing his cap from the peg, "I'd appreciate it. I'm not feeling very well."

He went home early to brace himself for Nilda's wrath.

-⟨⟨⟨◆⟩⟩⟩-

Aldama's wife spent weekday afternoons with her ninety-four-year-old mother, who'd been transferred to a nursing home in Yonkers. Nilda took the bus, because if Mama Freda had a rough day, she liked to stay at the home through dinner—and she no longer felt comfortable driving after dark. Later, when Aldama tried to reconstruct events in his mind, he remembered returning to the house, after picking up cigarettes at a convenience store, and watching the four o'clock news. At some point, he must have gone down to the cellar—he had no recollection of why— because that was where Nilda found him, shortly after seven o'clock, sprawled on the concrete. He'd suffered a stroke, fallen, and hit his head against the frame of the boiler. That was why the right side of his brain had been damaged, but the left side of his head throbbed. Or that, at least, was what the fast-talking doctor explained while testing his muscle tone.

He drifted off multiple times, a combination of the concussion and the morphine and the blood thinners, and finally awoke surrounded by his daughter, future son-in-law, and three of his four brothers. As he was adjusting to the hospital room, his wife entered, carrying a stack of bedding. "If you want something done well," she said to the ceiling, "do it yourself." But then she caught sight of Aldama, blinking against the unforgiving light, and declared, "It's about time you're awake." Her matter-of-fact tone couldn't conceal the swelling around her eyes.

"My head hurts," said Aldama. "Jesus Christ."

Hector, his oldest brother, echoed what the doctor had said earlier, through the haze, about the stroke and the fall. "Press this button for morphine," his brother said, sliding the PCA device into Aldama's right hand.

The barber opened and closed his fingers around the apparatus, relieved to find his muscles still worked. He lifted his arm from the bed with ease. He still had a trade, thank God—the Italian's words popped into his head. Only when he tried to elevate his left arm did it feel as though a heavy weight held down the limb. Nothing moved.

"You're going to be fine," said Nilda. "Now tell everybody you love them, so they can get home for supper and you can get some rest."

That was when he realized it was already the next evening—a full day was lost.

He hugged each of his brothers with his functional arm. Gloria kissed him on the forehead. Yet he was glad when they'd departed, upset that they'd seen him like this with tubes poking out of his neck and chest.

"I could have died," said Aldama. "And what about the business? Bernal won't know how to pay the bills."

"Don't think twice about the business," warned Nilda, fluffing his pillows. "Bernal has everything under control. He's family, remember. You can trust him."

Aldama trusted Bernal's honesty without question; his judgment was another matter entirely.

"He wanted to visit, but I wouldn't let him," added his wife. "You're not going to think about that shop again until you're done with rehab. I've already called about temporary disability. It's not much—and you should only be out six weeks—but you might as well get everything that you're entitled to."

And that's when the barber remembered Robustelli. In fact, Aldama recalled watching the four o'clock news the previous afternoon and wondering why the Italian wasn't eligible for Social Security payments: How had the hapless old man failed to earn even these most basic of protections? If he'd died, Aldama realized, his final thoughts would not have been about Nilda, or Gloria, but about the elderly Italian.

"I must tell you about Robustelli," he said.

Nilda held her finger to her lips. "Bernal told me already. It's not important," she said. "That's the problem with you, Adolfo. Mistaken priorities."

-≪◆≫-

Nilda proved true to her word. Over the next five weeks—both in the hospital and at the acute rehab facility—she refused to permit any mention of the barbershop. "You regain your strength," she said. "Right now, you let Bernal do the worrying." So it wasn't until the Sunday the barber returned home, able to walk aided only by a cane, that she even allowed her aunt's grandson to visit. Bernal had brought along his wife, baby daughter, and his parents, all crowded into Aldama's living room.

"So have you gone bankrupt yet?" Aldama asked.

"We're doing fine," the young man assured him. "I think you'll be very pleased with the receipts."

"And Robustelli?"

"I also hired someone on a temporary basis. Do you remember that heavy black woman from Queens? She's not half bad."

"So you've given away my chair already?" Aldama said, making the matter a joke for the benefit of the family. Secretly, he was annoyed. "I'm only gone six weeks, and I've already been replaced."

"Not *your* chair," Bernal corrected him. "Robustelli's."

Aldama felt a pang in his chest. "Don't tell me—"

"I didn't have a choice," said Bernal. "I discussed it with Auntie Nilda. He was going to scar somebody for life."

"Godammit," snapped Aldama. "You had no right."

He had wanted to say more, but his anger evaporated in a fit of coughing, and when he recovered, Nilda steered them all into the dining room for lunch.

-‹‹‹◆›››-

The next morning marked Aldama's return to the barbershop. All day long, he received well wishes, both from longtime customers and from local merchants. Get well cards lined the countertop. Steinhoff sent an arrangement of lilies. Yet the old Italian's absence—the harsh silence that replaced his colorful tales of Gable and Luciano—left the barber feeling his own age. He agreed with Bernal's assessment: Birdie wasn't half bad. But her semiconscious humming of show tunes made a poor substitute for regular encounters with the likes of Charlie Chaplin and Errol Flynn.

By midday, Aldama decided that he had to find Robustelli. Maybe he could pay the old man to look after the shop and to tell stories, he reflected—conjuring up a compromise that might both keep the Italian fed and the public safe. It was a crazy idea, true. And Nilda would accuse him of squandering their grandchildren's inheritance. But he would do it anyway, he decided. Because he wanted to—and because it was the right thing to do.

Tracking down Robustelli proved far more difficult than he'd anticipated. His first thought was to phone the old man, but he quickly realized he didn't know his phone number. Nor did he have a mailing address: they'd done all of their transactions in cash. Although he guessed the barber still lived in New York City, he couldn't even be sure which borough he inhabited. Ultimately, Aldama phoned both V. Robustellis in the telephone directory—one in the Bronx, the other on Staten Island—but neither number was correct. In desperation, he called other Robustellis—dozens of them—in the hope of locating a relative who might direct him to the missing barber. Alas, nobody had ever heard of the elderly Italian. His ads in *Barbers Only Magazine* and *Against The Grain* went unanswered. *If I could just apologize*, Aldama found himself thinking, *even that would be enough.*

The less hopeful he became of contacting Robustelli, the more Aldama found himself talking about the old man. "I used to work with another barber," he told a new customer one afternoon, "who'd clipped Clark Gable's mustache so he could play Fletcher Christian in *Mutiny on the Bounty.*" Aldama thought of Robustelli while he spoke—not the old man with the quaking arms, but the handsome youth smiling in the license photo. "And imagine this: Gable brought along a felt-lined jewelry box from Tiffany's to store the whiskers in. Just like setting an infant inside a casket. Now that's a story I'll never forget." Aldama told the story again the next morning, and others the following week. Eventually, he knew, he would leave out the part about another barber. Soon enough, one by one, the stories would all become his own.

BURROWING IN EXILE

-◄◄◄◆▶▶▶-

In my mother, the woodchuck found a fierce and steadfast ally.

My father's frustrations with the inexorable varmint came, over the years, to embody all of his life's disappointments—his stagnant career in public television, his ill-timed forays into the stock market, his unapologetically unremarkable daughter—but they proved no match for my mother's love of a fellow living creature. She'd yielded once, when he'd wanted to move from Manhattan to Laurendale, although Mama often described our upscale suburb as "a coffin with lawns"; she'd yielded again when my father opposed a second child: the exact expression he had apparently used was, "Let's quit while we're behind." Yet on the subject of glue traps for mice, and steel snares for raccoons, and, above all else, any of the lethal schemes my father hatched to rid his vegetable garden of the groundhog once and forever—many worthy of Rube Goldberg or Wile E. Coyote—my mother refused to bend. "If you hurt Mr. Whitman," Mama warned every June, calling the animal by one of her distinctive pet names, "I swear I'll take Molly and go to my sister's." By the summer I graduated from junior high school, I'd accepted this impasse—and the relentless bickering that accompanied it—as the price of love between two deeply incompatible people. So I was as shocked as Mama when, one July Fourth weekend, my father proposed a truce.

We were barbecuing that evening on the patio: my father painting garlic butter atop sirloin, while Mama charred squash and eggplant for herself on a separate section of the grill. Our mood was somber. Earlier that week, PBS had canceled production on "3-2-1-Cocktails," my father's effort to bring "the fine art of distilled spirits" to a national television audience. It was his second consecutive flop, following on the heels of "Cigar Chat" and leaving his future at the network uncertain. Out in the yard, rabbits scrambled to complete errands before nightfall. And then, as though to mock my father's failures, the woodchuck poked its shaggy brow from one of its countless burrows and ambled brazenly alongside the barbed fence that ringed the garden.

I braced for a slew of profanity. Instead, my father merely squeezed more juice from the steak with his spatula. "Let the bastard have his fun," he said. "I'm not getting myself worked up anymore over a damn whistle pig."

I glanced at my mother, who was preparing a lesson for her fifth graders. She raised her eyebrows, perplexed.

"It's too late to salvage anything this year," added my father. "Bastard's already taken the tops off all of my tomatoes and peppers. I know when I'm beat. But he'd better enjoy himself now, because this is the end of the gravy train."

"Warren?" When Mama said his name in this tone, her pitch rising like a dagger, it generally meant the onset of domestic warfare.

"Hear me out," said my father. "I got a ride to the station with Ed Sucram this morning—and somehow we ended up on the subject of gardening. He tells me there's a company that will relocate backyard pests without hurting them."

"Or so they claim," snapped my mother. "For all you know, they butcher the animals or abandon them in the gutter like roadkill."

"Nope. Not these guys. They're animal welfare nuts. Their varmints go to nature preserves or state parks. They'll even send you a photograph of the animal in its new habitat—for a small fee. I looked them up at work. They've got an A+ rating from the Better Business Bureau." My father served me a hunk of steak, then returned to the table with a bowl of baked potatoes wrapped in tinfoil. "Everybody wins, Jill. The whistle pig gets a safe new address free of cars and pesticides and exasperated green thumbs. And we get fresh, home-grown vegetables."

Mama eyed him warily. "But I *like* having Mr. Whitman around," she said. "Besides, what if he's homesick?"

"He has a brain the size of a walnut. How is he going to be homesick?"

"To tell you the truth, this makes me very nervous," answered Mama. "Our lawn is the only home the poor fellow has ever known."

"Come on, Jill," said my father. "I need some good news."

"I don't know what to tell you," said Mama. "Let's sleep on it."

My father finished his steak and potatoes in silence. Mama offered him a taste of her squash, but he shook his head. Her husband had grown up in a cramped cellar apartment, the child of Belgian refugees, and he valued the idea of home-grown produce far more than he actually liked eating it, much as he relished the idea of family vacations without enjoying long car rides or beaches or tourist attractions. His life's dream, I suppose, was to host dinner parties at which he would inform his A-list guests that he had hand-grown the salad on his own little patch of prosperity.

-⟪⟪◆⟫⟫-

The professional "relocator" from Rodent Holiday arrived three weeks later. His name was Jim. He was a lanky, pony-tailed guy in his early twenties—and he looked more like a college kid trying to fund a garage band than an "animal welfare nut." Above the knuckles of his right hand, he'd tattooed the letters l-e-f-t. His T-shirt, which hung loose over his torn jeans, depicted a cartoon rat, raccoon, and skunk—all laughing— beneath the caption: HAVEN'T THEY EARNED A VACATION? The company's box-truck sported prominent dents in both the front and rear fenders. Fortunately, after acquiescing to the move, Mama had gone to watch a

Broadway show with Aunt Phoebe. "If I have to see them taking him away," she'd said, "I know I'll have a breakdown."

Jim did not offer to shake my father's hand. Instead, he walked straight into the house—as though he'd just foreclosed on the place—and through the sliding doors onto the patio.

"Woodchuck, right?" he asked.

"I prefer whistle pig," said my father.

"Whatever," said Jim. "Do you know if it's a male or a female?"

"I really don't."

"Figures," answered Jim—and he flashed my father a look of disdain, as though any schoolchild could determine the gender of a groundhog at fifty paces. "In that case, we're going to have to use both sets of traps." He ran his fingers through his greasy hair. "There will be a surcharge."

The most efficient way to catch a woodchuck, it turned out, was with pheromones—but if you didn't know the gender of the creature in advance, you had to set up separate traps that gave off male and female scents. I waited with my father on the porch while the relocator laid out his wooden hutches in a semicircle and sprayed them with groundhog musk from a canister. Not that I gave a damn about the groundhog. But I was thirteen and desperately interested in Jeremy Allen, the sophomore lacrosse player whose parents lived catty-corner to our backyard. I fantasized that he would glimpse me through his window and duck across the hedgerows to say hello. Another two years would pass before I learned that broad-shouldered athletes didn't date plump girls with dull features, and another ten before I realized those plump, dull-featured girls hadn't missed much. But that balmy Sunday afternoon found me preening on the patio for a boy who wasn't looking, who probably wasn't even at home, while my father watched Jim romance his rodent nemesis with a nonexistent mate.

The seduction took nearly four hours. Mr. Whitman made multiple sorties toward the hutches, but developed cold feet every time. A black squirrel also poked around one of the traps, but quickly lost interest. My father paced the flagstones as though awaiting the birth of a baby. "Looks like you've got an indecisive one," said Jim. "Or maybe a bisexual." It sounded like an accusation—as though poor management on my father's part had muddled the groundhog's sexuality. When the creature finally succumbed to the aroma of lust, a grate sprang shut, letting Jim pick up the hutch by a handle. "It's a girl," he announced. "In case you were curious."

"Where are you taking her?" asked my father.

"Miami Beach" answered Jim.

"You serious?"

"As far as rodents are concerned, it's as good as Miami Beach," said Jim. "For a service fee, we can send you a photo." He draped a heavy canvas over the hutch; the animal hissed from within. "Buy the photo, dude. Trust me. Otherwise your wife will have you on the phone with us two months from now. I've seen it ten thousand times already."

I don't think anyone else—before or since—has ever called my father *dude*. Of course, the surest way to convince Warren Hagland *not* to do something was to advise him to do it.

"The last thing I want is a picture of that whistle pig," he said. "The minute it leaves here, I'm never thinking of it again."

"Suit yourself," said Jim.

The relocator had my father sign a release and gave him a carbon copy, then hoisted the cage atop his shoulder and vanished around the side of the house. He carried the animal with all the tenderness of a meatpacker.

My father placed his hand on my forearm—the closest he ever came to a gesture of tenderness. "The problem with your mother, Molly," he said, "is that she's sentimental. That's what happens when you grow up with wealthy parents. You don't think twice about sending your pests to Miami Beach or Disneyworld or the honeymoon suite at the Waldorf-Astoria." His face looked genuinely pained. "If it were up to me, we could have done the job with a handful of strychnine pellets—and then *told* people we'd arranged to have the whistle pig flown to the Riviera or wherever."

A flock of mourning doves skimmed over the peonies, settling on the burrow-scarred grass that bounded the garden. I gazed at the small birds across the naked lawn, and suddenly, I felt a pang of loss for the departed woodchuck.

-«««•»»»-

I cannot ever remember my father—before or since—in as good spirits as he was those first few weeks after Mr. Whitman's departure to "Rodent Miami Beach." He doubled my allowance that evening, adding a twenty-dollar one-time bonus. He kissed my mother on the forehead at the breakfast table the following morning, and each subsequent morning, a gesture that had evaporated years earlier. At night, through the sheer wall between our bedrooms, I heard the unfamiliar sounds of their intimacy. My father even raised the prospect of adopting a puppy, although the plan never advanced beyond a scouting trip to the local ASPCA shelter. What was most amazing about my father's good cheer was that, on paper, his life was unraveling.

I'd overheard Mama unburdening herself to Aunt Phoebe on the telephone, so I knew that my father had been "reassigned" at work, which was basically a face-saving demotion, and that the personal checks he'd written to keep "3-2-1-Cocktails" afloat had largely wiped out our family savings. Two days after he paid to relocate the woodchuck, he'd been forced to cash out his retirement fund to meet our delinquent property tax bill. And yet after work every evening, he wandered the backyard with his arms folded across his chest, poking his boot tips into the groundhog's abandoned holes and beaming. By the following weekend, he was promising fresh tomatoes and eggplants to the neighbors—a year in advance.

"It's not just about the damn whistle pig," he declared as he flipped hamburgers on the grill. "It's about having control of one's destiny. Honestly, Jill, we should have done this years ago. Live and learn." He took a deep breath, savoring the twilight; the air smelled of maple pollen and sizzling beef. "I'm going to invite Ed and Terri Sucram over next week to celebrate," he said.

"I'm glad you're so happy," replied Mama. "But to tell you the truth, I actually miss the little fellow."

"You're a crazy person," said my father.

"Gee, thanks."

"You're welcome, crazy person," he said—and then he wrapped his arms around her waist from behind and ran his lips up the side of her neck.

For a fleeting moment, my parents were once again the affectionate couple preserved on 35-mm slides of their European honeymoon. They'd met on the set of my father's first production—my mother had a college internship at the studio—and he'd asked her out a dozen times over several months before she finally agreed to a date. Even in grade school, I remember wondering what had made Mama yield. She was already struggling with her weight back then, so I guess she didn't have many offers. But in the wake of the woodchuck's departure, it was possible to imagine more than acquiescence between them—to see them as love-blind and enraptured. And if my father could fall for my mother, I told myself, Jeremy Allen could as easily fall for me.

Three days later, before my father had an opportunity to display his woodchuck-free lawn to the Sucrams, the first of the letters arrived. He'd picked me up from one of my summer babysitting gigs on the way home from work that evening—Mama, the quintessential Manhattanite, still hadn't learned how to drive after nine years in suburbia—and, as I had raced to retrieve the day's mail from the curbside box, secretly hoping for a love note from Jeremy, I was the first to handle the letter. It arrived in a standard business envelope, bearing a first-class stamp postmarked Pontefract, my father's name and address printed in firm block letters. In the upper left-hand corner, the return address read simply WOODCHUCK. I placed the strange envelope on the kitchen table along with the day's slew of bills and charitable solicitations. When my father opened it, several minutes later, he actually grinned.

"Very funny," he said. He slid the letter across the table to my mother. "I don't suppose you know anything about this."

I read the letter over my mother's shoulder.

Dear Mr. Hagland:

   I do not imagine you expected to hear from me again, and I am sorry to burden you with my problems, but I am in desperate need of help and I do not know where else to turn.

   I am lonely and homesick and miss the life we shared in our yard. If you can find it in your heart to take me back, I will be forever grateful.

Sincerely,

Woodchuck

PS: This place is nothing like Miami Beach.

   Firm block letters in black ink. The nondescript handwriting reminded me of the ransom requests from television mysteries.

   Mama did not find the note amusing. "You don't think he's actually homesick?" she asked. "I mean: this is obviously a gag, but that doesn't mean there isn't any underlying truth."

   An uncomfortable silence descended upon the kitchen, punctuated only by the hum of the refrigerator. I could sense the gears churning inside my father's head as he struggled to contain his frustration. "I thought we had put this business behind us," he finally said. "Now I want a straight answer, Jill. Yes or no. Did you or didn't you have anything to do with this letter?"

   "Absolutely nothing," replied my mother. "Sorry to disappoint you."

   Pontefract was a bedroom community several towns away. In order to mail a letter from there, my mother would have had to change busses twice.

   "Are you sure you didn't write it yourself?" asked Mama. "Maybe you're weighed down by unconscious guilt and you wrote it in your sleep."

   My father ignored her. "I don't need this," he said. He crumpled the letter into a ball and deposited it in the kitchen garbage. "I suppose it could be Carl Henry's wife. She didn't seem so thrilled when I told them about the relocation."

   Dr. and Mrs. Henry lived next door to Jeremy Allen. It was hard to imagine her taking time away from her two-year-old twins to impersonate a groundhog, but I understood that nothing good would come from voicing an opinion.

"I knew this was a bad idea," said Mama. "Can you call the company and ask them how Mr. Whitman is doing? I thought they were supposed to send a picture."

"I could," answered my father. "But I won't. I'm done with this, Jill. If you want a picture, Molly can draw you a picture."

–≪≪◆≫≫–

But my father was far from done with the woodchuck.

Another letter arrived the next day, and then another, and another, until retrieving the rodent missives became a part of my afternoon routine. I'd finish babysitting for the Garbers or the Pastarnacks or the Arcayas in the early evening, then my father would drive me home and I'd retrieve the rodent's correspondence for him. All of the envelopes came from Pontefract, painstakingly block-lettered. In each, "the woodchuck" pleaded for assistance in returning to our yard. I CANNOT COME BACK ON MY OWN, wrote the author. I DO NOT KNOW THE ROUTE. In one letter, the creature described her efforts to conceal herself in the rear of a gardener's truck, hoping to comb the neighborhood for familiar landmarks—but the Portuguese driver discovered her and sprayed her down with a hose. In another, she wrote of missing her baby sister and nieces, who apparently lived beneath the azalea beds of Mrs. Steinhoff down the block. Increasingly, the letters darkened my father's mood. He even wrote "return to sender" on one unopened envelope, but the postman refused to accept it—as "Woodchuck, Pontefract" was not a valid address. By the third week of daily letters, my parents had returned to their chronic squabbling and contempt.

"If I find out you're behind this—either of you—I swear I'll—," my father threatened one evening over supper.

"You'll what?" demanded Mama.

"Whistle pigs don't write letters," said my father. I had heard him pacing the veranda for several nights, as he'd done before Mr. Whitman's relocation, and his face wore the haggard look of rumpled pillow. "Someone—some human being—is behind this. And it's harassment. And I don't have to take it anymore."

Forty-five minutes later, a young female officer from the Laurendale Police Department was seated in our dining room. She had a chubby face, but carried her weight well, and she wore a wedding ring; her fingernails, trimmed short, were lacquered fuchsia. As she read through the most recent letter, I could tell that she was biting her lip. My father and I sat opposite her; from the kitchen drifted the sound of my mother clearing dishes.

"You say you've discarded all of the others?" asked the officer.

She flipped open a leather-bound notepad.

"It was a mistake," said my father. "I'll keep them from now on."

"What makes you so sure you'll be getting more of them?"

The officer's voice brimmed with suspicion. Maybe she actually did think that my father was sending himself mail. After all, people do some rather crazy things during domestic disputes.

"I'm not sure," said my father. "Obviously, if you can stop them, you won't hear any complaints from me."

"Anybody have a grudge against you?" asked the officer.

A comprehensive answer could have filled her entire pad. My father's existence was a long series of skirmishes over finances and property lines and perceived social slights. *I'm sorry* simply wasn't part of his vocabulary. His own sister—my Aunt Angela—wasn't on speaking terms with him.

"Minor disagreements now and then," he said. "Nothing like this."

"And your marriage? How is it between you and your wife?"

"It is just dandy between me and my wife," said my father—imitating the officer's diction. "All peaches and cream."

"I'm sorry," replied the officer. "I have to ask."

"So you asked. Now what are you going to do about the letters?"

"Can't help you there, I'm afraid," said the officer. "There's nothing threatening here. Nothing obscene. It's probably some teenager playing a prank. The best thing to do is to ignore him until he tires himself out."

"And what if he doesn't?" demanded my father. "Can't you trace them?"

The officer returned her pad to her duty belt. "Obviously, if the letters do become threatening, you should let us know immediately," she said.

She smiled at me. "Anything to add, young lady?"

I shrugged. "I like your nails," I said.

"Thanks, honey," said the officer. She turned to my father: "If you want my personal opinion, Mr. Hagland, I think you're far too worked up over this. If this isn't a prank—if someone really harbors a grudge against you— you're giving him exactly what he wants." She lowered her voice. "If *I* was getting these letters," she added, "I wouldn't even bother to open them."

The officer was hardly out the door when my father's criticism started. "Did you really have to comment on her fingernails?" he demanded. "Honestly, Molly, if you're not going to say anything helpful, you ought to learn not to say anything at all."

"But she asked."

"And you had to answer?"

At that instant, Mama stepped into the foyer. "Are you two fighting?"

"I'm just giving your daughter some helpful advice," said my father. "So she doesn't make a fool of herself in the future."

"It sounded like fighting to me," said Mama. "What did the cop say?"

"Nothing useful. Lazy bitch," grumbled my father.

"Nice language." My mother, still wearing her cooking gloves, sat down next to me on the stairs and gave me a hug. "Why don't you do everyone a favor, Warren, including yourself, and have them bring back the groundhog? Honestly, you wouldn't be so upset about the letters if you didn't feel guilty."

"Nobody feels guilty, goddammit." He cupped his fist in his palm. "Jesus Christ, Jill," he shouted. "I can't believe you want the damn whistle pig to win."

My father stepped out onto the front porch and slammed the door behind him, sending a shudder through the woodwork. The house still felt like it was reverberating from the blow ten minutes later, when he rang the bell. He'd forgotten his key.

-««•»»-

Another two weeks of letters arrived before my father called Rodent Holiday. I can't say for certain whether he was driven by guilt or exasperation or an irrational fear that the woodchuck was actually writing him letters. What I do know is the man who picked up the telephone that evening, his cheeks dark with five o'clock shadow, the flavor of cognac heavy on his breath, was a shadow of the creature who'd criticized me for complimenting the policewoman on her fingernails. He'd avoided opening the letters from Pontefract for three straight days, but eventually he gave in, and I suppose reading the three pleas in succession proved enough to unmoor him. "You win, Jill. You win, and the whistle pig wins, and everyone wins except me," he cried as he searched the yellow pages for the relocator's number. "To hell with fresh tomatoes. I just want to put this bullshit behind me."

"Hello? Rodent Holiday?" he said. "May I speak to Jim?"

Unfortunately for my father, Jim no longer worked at Rodent Holiday.

"So, look," he explained to one of Jim's replacements, "I had you guys relocate a woodchuck from my property in early July, and now I want her back."

My father twirled the phone cord between his fingers.

"No, I don't have a photograph," he said. "Yes, I do realize I could have purchased a photograph for a small fee."

The exchange deteriorated from there. The relocators were willing to *attempt* to retrieve Mr. Whitman—for twice what it had cost to remove her—but they couldn't make any promises. In the wild, woodchucks faced all sorts of hazards: septic tanks, organophospates, predation from hawks and foxes and domestic cats. According to Rodent Holiday, the odds were 50-50 that Mr. Whitman was already dead. My father did not inform them that he was corresponding with the animal.

"What a racket," he groused. "Six weeks ago, they were sending the whistle pig to Miami Beach. All of a sudden, it's like they sent the bastard to Siberia." He crossed to the sideboard and poured himself another glass of cognac. "It's price gouging. I swear I should report the assholes to the state's attorney general."

Yet my father was nothing but grateful when the box truck from Rodent Holiday pulled into our driveway three days later. Our new agent, a morbidly obese thirty-something named Chet, sported a ragged T-shirt from "Fat Kids: The Musical." He flashed me the knowing and too-familiar smile that overweight girls come to expect from lonely, overweight men. "One female groundhog," he announced, removing the canvas from the hutch with a flourish. "Dinner is served."

My father examined the creature cautiously, one hand jiggling coins in his pocket. He did not smile. I avoided eye contact with the relocator.

"That was a joke," said Chet. "I know you're not going to eat her."

"She doesn't look right," said my father. "How do you know this is *our* woodchuck? You could just be bringing me some random animal."

Chet laughed—a high pitched squeal. "We keep careful track of where we deposit the cargo," he explained. "We picked up your woodchuck only yards from where we left her. Now I can't *prove* this is your animal, but the odds are strongly in favor of it. Needless to say, Rodent Holiday makes no guarantees."

"Of course, it doesn't." My father held up his thumb and index finger in front of the hutch as though he were measuring the woodchuck. "She looks kind of small. Can you at least tell me *where* you deposit your cargo?"

"I'm sorry, sir, but that I cannot do. Proprietary secret."

My father inspected the woodchuck again. He even poked his index finger between the bars of the hutch, but withdrew it quickly at the groundhog's approach.

"Okay, we'll take her."

Chet mopped perspiration from his broad forehead with the bottom of his shirt, revealing his bare paunch in the process. "That will be cash only," he said. "No refunds or exchanges." After my father paid him—retrieving the money from my mother's pocketbook—he opened the hutch; the woodchuck ambled onto the yard. Then Chet turned to me and asked, "Do you want to see the raccoons and the badgers? I got a whole batch of cargo in the truck."

"No, she doesn't," answered my father.

Chet eyed me with sympathy. I didn't want to be rude, but the thought crossed my mind that Jeremy Allen might see us together—and I ran into the house without another word. From the bay windows, I watched as the relocator's truck vanished around Mrs. Steinhoff's rhododendrons, and then as my father followed the groundhog in her jaunt across the grass. I couldn't help noticing that—like pet owners who grow to resemble their dogs or cats—my father and his rodent nemesis had somehow acquired similar manners of walking.

When the mail arrived the next afternoon, none of us were surprised to encounter another envelope postmarked Pontefract. Mr. Whitman had likely mailed the letters several days earlier, my father reassured himself. Nor was he particularly alarmed on day two or day three. But the letter that arrived on day four actually drove my father to tears. He sat at the kitchen table, weeping in frustration, while I read the letter aloud to Mama.

Dear Mr. Hagland:

A truck from rodent holiday arrived this morning, and I hope you can understand how this raised my expectations. Alas, Mr. Chet carried off one of the woodchucks who lives in a nearby burrow.

Nevertheless, this incident gives me hope that it is possible to return to my home once again.

Sincerely,

Woodchuck

PS: The forage here is awful. I miss your glorious tomatoes and peppers.

It impressed me how much the letter actually sounded like the voice of a groundhog.

"If I ever find out who's behind this," said my father, "I swear I won't be responsible for my actions." He lit a cigarette—the first cigarette I'd seen him smoke in several years; the smoke drifted toward the skylight like a plea for help. "You don't think that company is sending these, do you? As part of some scam?"

Mama opened the window, letting in the muggy August air. "I thought they had an A+ rating from the Better Business Bureau."

"Fuck their rating. I swear I'm getting our damn whistle pig back." My father pounded his fist on the Formica tabletop, rattling the vase that my mother kept freshly stocked with forsythias. "I don't give a rat's ass how much it costs. I don't give a rat's ass if I have to stake out their fucking office and follow them to their cargo deposits. You two may not care if we're publicly humiliated, but I'm not going to stand for it."

-⫷⫷◆⫸⫸-

Since Rodent Holiday refused to exchange the new woodchuck, and since my parents were running short on cash, my father decided against relocating the unwanted creature before he made another attempt to lure back Mr. Whitman. "What's the difference between one whistle pig or two?" he demanded. "Or ten for that matter? Let *them* fight over vegetables for a change." So when Chet arrived with another female groundhog the following Monday, our rodent population doubled. But the desperate letters kept coming. By the third week of August, we were up to four groundhogs. The creatures sunned themselves in the yard, or scampered playfully in the chrysanthemums, seemingly oblivious to the strife they were causing inside our house. My mother made the mistake of observing the four animals could play a hand of contract bridge—and my father threw his brandy snifter into the plate glass window, shattering both. When Chet arrived with the fifth woodchuck, the elderly Italian lady who lived next door watched us doubtfully from the head of her driveway. Earlier, she'd complained to my parents that their "menagerie" was grazing on her tea roses.

"So this is your last chance, Mr. Hagland," said Chet.

He displayed yet another caged female woodchuck. I followed the proceedings from behind the bay window curtains.

My father frowned. "What's that supposed to mean?"

"We're closing up shop for the autumn soon," said the relocator. "But more importantly, my boss says we can't keep bringing cargo *into* a residential neighborhood."

"You cannot be serious," objected my father. "There must be ten gazillion whistle pigs in this neighborhood—and you're afraid to bring in one more. This is total bullshit. I should sue the pants off you for discrimination."

Chet endured this abuse impassively. He held the final hutch in one hand; his other tiny hand rested on his paunch. I knew I should feel compassion for the poor guy, but I found myself despising him.

"Maybe you'll get lucky this time, sir," he said.

"Maybe you should mind your own business," answered my father. "You better hope you've got the right varmint—or you'll be hearing from my lawyers."

The creature who exited the hutch was not promising. She looked far scrawnier than Mr. Whitman had—and she favored her left side when she walked, as though she'd suffered a stroke in her absence. Since Labor Day was fast approaching, several of my babysitting gigs dried up, so over the next few days, I was able to watch the crippled animal from the patio. It crossed my mind that Rodent Holiday wasn't retrieving groundhogs from their original destinations at all—it was merely bringing us animals relocated from other yards. For all we knew, they circulated groundhogs from community to community in a giant rodent Ponzi operation.

"It's her," said my father. "I'm sure it's her."

"Don't count your groundhogs," warned Mama.

"Screw you," snapped my father. "I'll count what I want to count."

When the mail arrived the following afternoon, I was waiting to retrieve the letter emblazoned WOODCHUCK from the box. My father took the envelope—unopened—and burned it with a match over the kitchen sink. He did the same with Wednesday's letter. And Thursday's. But on Friday, for the first time in two months, we received nothing postmarked Pontefract. By Saturday, without another rodent missive, my father was ready to celebrate. He bought six pounds of choice tenderloin and fired up the grill. My mother went to the movies with her sister.

Out in the yard, our five woodchucks engaged in various feats of rodentine gymnastics and frolic. One was supposedly Mr. Whitman, while the others were impostors, but it was impossible to tell them apart.

"Look at that, Molly," said my father. "There's a lesson in all this. Winning is important—damn important—but it's also important to be flexible." He spread discount barbecue sauce atop our expensive steak. "Your mother means well, but she's not goal oriented. That's the difference between us. I want to be remarkable. She's willing to settle for mediocre. Now that you're old enough to start thinking about your future, you should be asking yourself, Do I want to be remarkable? Or am I going to settle for something less?"

That was the last time I remember my father happy, in those final days before he lost his grip on the future. My parents would be separated within three months; by year's end, the Laurendale house—woodchucks and all—would be sold to a developer and divided into flag-lots. I'd never date Jeremy Allen; in fact, after I moved back to the city with my mother, I never saw him again. But that evening, looking out at the cheerful groundhogs cavorting in the twilight, I didn't regret those long bus trips to Pontefract or the pocket money I lost on fewer babysitting hours. To this day, writing those letters is the only truly remarkable thing that I have ever done.

TRACKING HAROLD LLOYD

-«««◊»»»-

Maybe because her own grandmothers are both long dead, Meredith's nine-year-old daughter takes an immediate shine to Mrs. Rolleston. Lauren calls her their "new, old neighbor": new because they have lived in Hager Hills only three days, old because the turbaned woman rocking on the nearby porch appears to be camped at death's doorstep. Meredith watches from the far side of the azalea hedge as Lauren speaks with the elderly lady, then listens as her daughter rehashes their conversation. It's nearly eight o'clock—a humid summer twilight—and they're waiting to welcome Lauren's father home from his shift at the hospital.

"Mr. Harold Lloyd's gone missing," reports Lauren. "That's why Mrs. Rolleston looks so sad. She's been waiting for him to come home."

"Oh, I see," says Meredith.

"Mr. Harold Lloyd is the same age as I am. Only in people years, that's . . . " Lauren reflects for a moment and demands, "What's nine times seven?"

"Sixty-three."

"Mr. Harold Lloyd is sixty-three in human years. Can we help find him?" A flash of insight strikes the girl and she adds, "*Please.*"

Meredith glances over the hedge at her ancient neighbor, whose peculiar chiffon robe and matching silk headpiece recall the matinee idols of a bygone era. The old woman acknowledges her with a nod. What choice does she have but to cross the narrow swath of lawn between their properties and introduce herself? If she doesn't break the ice now, Meredith realizes, she never will. Lauren races ahead of her.

"I hear you've lost your dog," says Meredith.

"He'll come back," replies Mrs. Rolleston. "Always does. Finest companion I've ever had. Loyal as the day is long."

Lauren has already mounted the old lady's porch and perches behind her chair, the girl's slender arms folded like a security guard's across her chest. "Show my mom the pictures," she urges.

"Yes, the pictures." Mrs. Rolleston reaches into her oversized handbag and withdraws a plastic chain of photo inserts. All but one—of a dapper young man in Navy uniform—depict dogs. "That's Mr. Buster Keaton," she says, pointing to a sepia-tone print of an Irish setter. "I couldn't have been older than your daughter when Papa brought him home." Next come Polaroids, preserving the images of canines "Mr. Charlie Chaplin" and "Mr. Ben Turpin" and "Mr. Fatty Arbuckle." Finally, they arrive at the chocolate merle collie named after the Jazz Age comedian du jour. Mr. Harold Lloyd poses before a concrete water fountain.

"How long has he been missing?"

Mrs. Rolleston frowns at Meredith as though fearing a trick question. "Let me see . . . Three days. Three or four. I didn't start worrying until this morning."

"Mom says we can help you find him," chimes in Lauren. "We'll put up signs and knock on doors."

Dog tracking hadn't been on Meredith's agenda for the week—she still has nearly an entire house to uncrate before her teaching duties begin at the middle school—but how can she repudiate her own daughter's altruism? Besides, she genuinely feels for their "new, old neighbor."

"That would be just darling of you," says Mrs. Rolleston. "If it's not too much trouble, that is. I don't know what I'll do if my baby doesn't come home."

"We'll find Mr. Harold Lloyd," insists Lauren. "I promise."

-◄◄◄◆►►►-

Meredith is no stranger to missing dogs. She lost two of her own as a girl: a terrier named Walrus to a downed electrical wire and a one-eyed mutt called Blackie to a speeding delivery truck. The primary reason they've relocated to Hager Hills from Brooklyn is to protect Lauren from such misfortunes—not just hit-and-run pet killers, but stray bullets and PCP dealers and sex predators vending shaved ice. In suburbia, Meredith reassures herself, eccentric old ladies are just that—eccentric, not evil—and escaped border collies return of their own accord. Surely, it's a good sign that her daughter wishes to devote the final days of summer break to stapling flyers onto telephone poles. Lauren has always been an introverted child—slow to warm up, reluctant to let go. Like Meredith herself at that age, she reflects. Like Meredith *still*. So the girl's sudden friendship with Edith Rolleston also appears promising.

The next morning, they scan Mr. Harold Lloyd's photograph into Albert's hospital-issued computer and print up five hundred wanted posters:

MISSING!!!!
Mr. Harold Lloyd
nine years old
(sixty-three in human years)
Phone 914-555-0185 (before 10 pm only)

The final caveat is included at Mrs. Rolleston's insistence. "It won't kill someone to look after my baby overnight," she declares. "I've been unplugging my telephone at precisely ten o'clock for forty years, and I see no reason to stop today. Besides, that's well after Mr. Harold Lloyd's bedtime." Meredith forces herself to take these quirks in stride, striving to appear easygoing for Lauren's sake. She has read in one of her "how-to-parent" guides—the ones that Albert constantly mocks—that the best way to overcome her daughter's social anxiety is to conceal her own.

Once they secure Mrs. Rolleston's blessing for their flyers, they affix them to every lamppost and mailbox and street sign within a ten-block radius. The day grows warm, but not too warm, and deathly still. Seemingly all of Hager Hills has escaped to distant offices or summer camps or beach cottages along the Connecticut shore, leaving only the pair of them and homebound Mrs. Rolleston to guard the town. Unfortunately, Mrs. Rolleston's bungalow stands at the end of their cul-de-sac; on the far side of her yard, past the makeshift canine burial ground where crude stone mounds honor "Mr. Charlie Chaplin" and his offspring, acres of unkempt woodland form a perimeter around an upscale golf club. Meredith suspects that Mr. Harold Lloyd has vanished into this undergrowth. If so, he is beyond the aid of a tenacious nine-year-old and an overweight middle school teacher.

By noon, they've exhausted the flyers.

"Now we have to ring doorbells," announces Lauren.

Ringing doorbells is out of character for Meredith's daughter—a girl so fearful of strangers that she once pleaded not to go trick-or-treating. *Well within the realm of normal*, the school's psychologist had counseled. *Give her time to gain her sea legs.* . . . Yet Meredith has had thirty-seven years to acquire her own "sea legs" and she still finds parent-teacher conferences worse than a night on the rack. If it were up to her headshrinker husband, they'd both be on high doses of Zoloft.

"I saved one flyer," explains Lauren. "To show people."

Of course, there are few people around in Hager Heights to show at midday on a Tuesday. The first three bells Lauren rings go unanswered. At the fourth house, the red brick colonial at the corner of Pontefract Street, a round-faced Indian woman of about fifty opens the door. She sports a turquoise *kameez* over her loose-fitting *shalwar*, a red tilaka graces her forehead. "I can help you?" she asks.

Lauren says nothing. She merely stands mute, as though pierced silent by a toxic arrow, until the Indian woman looks to Meredith for guidance. If not for her daughter, Meredith knows she might run off herself without speaking.

"Our neighbor's dog is missing," she says. "You haven't seen him, have you?"

The homeowner shakes her head. "You think I see your dog, I *keep* it?" She sounds incredulous. "Most certainly, I see your dog, I give it back."

"We just thought . . . ," says Meredith—but suddenly she feels like a fool. She rests her palms on Lauren's shoulders and discovers the girl is trembling. "I'm sorry."

"It is okay," responds the woman, now smiling. "I keep eyes open for dog."

Then the door closes and Meredith stands alone on the walk, hugging her daughter. "We don't need to go house-to-house to find him," she says. "Oh, honey."

—«‹•›»—

Mrs. Rolleston invites them into her kitchen for iced tea later that afternoon to thank them for their efforts. The interior of the old woman's home looks like a storeroom at a museum: cardboard boxes line both sides of the entryway, brimming over with glassware and books. In the foyer, colorful figurines of leprechauns and dwarves elbow for space atop a gateleg table. Meredith notes the burnt-out bulbs in the chandeliers, the rotary wall telephone alongside the refrigerator. She can't help thinking of the mess that awaits inside her own kitchen—the lawn chairs stacked in the dining room—the clean clothing piled high on the carpet beside their bed. The tea itself, which Mrs. Rolleston serves in tall, frosted glasses, tastes far too sweet.

Mrs. Rolleston does not drink iced tea. Instead, she pours herself a glass of orange juice and tops it off with a shot of Canadian whiskey. "Papa swore the key to a long life was a thimbleful of spirits every afternoon— and he lived to be ninety-three, so there must be something to it." She sits down opposite them at the kitchen table, sweeping aside stacks of unopened mail. "My father trained dogs for Warner Brothers: Strongheart; Jean, the Vitagraph Dog; four generations of Rin Tin Tins. He'd been a bank teller in Philadelphia, but when we moved to Los Angeles, he told everyone he was a licensed veterinarian—and they believed him." The tale that ensues features encounters with Cecil B. DeMille and Mary Pickford and culminates in a romance between Olivia de Havilland's poodle and Errol Flynn's German shepherd. Meredith has no idea whether any of it is actually true. What interests her most is that her daughter, who knows nothing of these faded stars, never once takes her eyes off the storyteller. Why Lauren is not self-conscious around this elderly lady proves a mystery, just like why most other strangers terrify her. "I have a picture somewhere of me with the real Mr. Harold Lloyd," says Mrs. Rolleston. "Quite a nice snapshot."

"Can I see it?" asks Lauren.

"I'll have to find it. That's the problem with living alone in such a big house."

Meredith glances at her watch. It is already four o'clock.

"We should be going, honey," she says. "I'm sure Mrs. Rolleston has other obligations besides showing us pictures."

"Nonsense. I'm glad for the company."

So they wait at the kitchen table while their host searches for the photograph—first in the foyer, later upstairs. They hear floorboards creaking overhead. Meredith contemplates calling out to the elderly woman, explaining that they really must leave, but she doesn't have the heart. An intense sadness settles over her. How fortunate she is to have Lauren, to have Albert—to have *something* other than a dimly lit house crammed with worthless heirlooms. More than an hour slips away before the old lady returns, empty-handed.

"I suppose I must have left it behind in California. I'm sorry."

"It's all right," says Meredith, rising. "Thank you for the tea."

She glares pointedly at her daughter. "Thank you for the tea," echoes Lauren.

Their host insists upon escorting them to the front door. Mrs. Rolleston's gait is hunched and painstakingly slow, as though she carries an animal carcass on her back.

"You'll call us if you hear anything about Mr. Harold Lloyd?" asks Lauren.

It takes a moment for Meredith to register she means the dog, not the lost photo.

"Immediately," agrees Mrs. Rolleston, blowing kisses with her gloved hands. "And thank you, darling. Thank you both."

As soon as they're back on their own porch, Lauren asks: "Can we get a puppy?"

—⟨⟨⟨◆⟩⟩⟩—

Nobody answers the flyers. Mrs. Rolleston's only visitors are the postman and the van from her grocery service. At first, Meredith is able to distract her daughter with other tasks—shelving books and linens, polishing her late mother-in-law's silver. By Friday morning, Lauren practically welds herself to the telephone, in case Mrs. Rolleston calls to report that Mr. Harold Lloyd has been found. Every time a vehicle passes, the girl hurries to the bay windows in the living room and pulls back the drapes. The upshot of these antics is that Meredith—who prefers to feign absence when strangers ring their doorbell—can't pretend that she isn't home, and she finds herself forced to accept housewarming gifts from three different neighbors. Two bottles of Chablis, one of Zinfandel. (Later, Albert discovers that the Zinfandel has been regifted and that the original card still lies taped to the bottle.) *You should have a house warming party*, each woman urges. The chitchat borders on torture. Eventually, Meredith makes the mistake of sharing with Lauren her fears regarding the dog.

"Honestly, honey, I don't think anyone is going to find him," she says. "It's already been a full week. Mr. Harold Lloyd is probably out in those woods somewhere."

Dead in those woods, she thinks to herself—but she doesn't dare say it.

"I bet he can't find his way home," contends Lauren. "We'll have to rescue him."

Meredith knows that a rescue mission is an ill-advised idea—that they are as likely to stumble upon Mr. Harold Lloyd's cadaver as they are to find a living dog—but Lauren is now tugging at her arms with desperation. She is actually about to yield when the girl releases her grasp. "Fine, I'll go myself," cries her daughter. And seconds later, the girl has disappeared through the kitchen door and down the back steps. By the time Meredith reaches the edge of Mrs. Rolleston's yard, all she can see through the brush is a distant patch of blue denim.

"Please, honey!" cries Meredith. "At least, wait for me."

She wades into the sea of tangled vines, holding her arms above her shoulders to avoid thorns and poison ivy. Her sandals sink through the decaying leaves below. The rich, fecund smells of the forest tickles her nostrils. "Hold on! I'm coming."

"Okay, I'm waiting," answers Lauren. "But come quick."

Meredith swats away branches, inching her way toward her daughter's blue dungarees and carmine top. Her worst fear is that Lauren will encounter the dog's corpse without her, as she once found Walrus's body lifeless on the sidewalk. "I'm almost there," she calls out—but too late. Without warning, the blue and red patches sweep like frightened animals across the foliage.

"I hear him!" screams Lauren. "I hear him!"

At first, Meredith hears nothing, just the low-pitched murmur of the countryside. But then, all at once, the sound reaches her too. Barking. The deep, resonant tones of the collie's voice are unmistakable. She also hears her daughter thrashing through the underbrush in hot pursuit of the dog. Up until this moment, the animal has been only a secondary consideration for Meredith—important to her merely because it is important to Lauren—but now saving Mr. Harold Lloyd takes on an urgency of its own.

Meredith picks up her speed until she finds herself charging blindly through brambles and thickets. A twig catches her in the eye; she nearly turns an ankle. Yet she pushes forward, even as her lungs run short of breath. Ahead of her, the dog continues to bark—and now her daughter is calling out his name. "Mr. Harold Lloyd! Come, Harold! HAROLD!!!" reverberates through the oaks and hickories.

She scrambles over a mossy log and emerges at the edge of the golf course, onto a gravel path that hugs the surrounding chain-link fence. Beyond the angle in the fence, she still hears the dog—and then, like the whir of a bullet, a whistle. A moment later, Meredith stands face to face with the whistler and his dog.

The dog's fur appears all white, except for a triangular black patch atop its crown. Maybe a Samoyed or a small husky. Certainly no border collie. He yaps wildly at the root of a nearby maple. The creature's owner, a bare-chested teenager, carries a Frisbee under his elbow; his T-shirt dangles from the belt of his trousers. "Knock it off, Fillmore," commands the teenager. Lingering about twenty yards away from the boy and his companion, Meredith's daughter wears an anguished expression.

"It's okay," says the teen. "He's friendly."

Lauren rushes to Meredith and collapses tearfully against her chest.

-«««◆»»»-

They retreat to Mrs. Rolleston's kitchen for another round of iced tea. An entire box of Oreo cookies helps the girl shed her disappointment. "We couldn't expect to rescue him on our first search," Lauren assures their host. "But we'll try again after lunch. If we divide the woods into squares, we'll definitely find him." Meredith takes pride in her daughter's reasoning, even as she laments the effort such a search may entail.

"Well, I thank you for looking, darling. You can't imagine how much good a bit of neighborly kindness does a person," says Mrs. Rolleston. "That's what it used to be like everywhere when I was your age. Even in

Hollywood. Did I ever tell you about the time Lionel Barrymore climbed a tree after my sister's cat?"

To Meredith's daughter, Lionel Barrymore could as easily be the King of Siam—but that does nothing to dampen her interest.

"Do you have a picture?" Lauren asks.

"Oh, I don't think so. It was Lizzie's cat, not mine," replies Mrs. Rolleston, sipping what Meredith notes to be her second juice-and-whiskey of the morning. "But I do have a photograph of Mr. Harold Lloyd somewhere—a nice picture, in front of a water fountain. I haven't shown it to you, have I?"

And instantly, Meredith knows there is no dog.

Maybe Mr. Harold Lloyd has been missing for months, or years, or quite possible, he's resting under one of those crude stone mounds at the cusp of the woods. But he might as easily be buried beneath a freeway ramp in Southern California. At the same time, Meredith knows that there must be a dog—that a lost dog is tragic, but a nonexistent dog is far more devastating. Even if he only exists for a homebound old woman and a nine-year-old girl, and briefly within the imagination of an overweight middle school teacher, there must be a dog named Harold Lloyd lost somewhere in the woods, and that she will spend the final days of summer break searching for him.

"I did show you, didn't I?" asks Mrs. Rolleston.

"Show us again," says Lauren.

Mrs. Rolleston reaches into her handbag and fans out the chain of plastic-encased snapshots. "This one's Mr. Fatty Arbuckle," she says, "And this one's Mr. Harold Lloyd." Lauren beams with pleasure; Meredith smiles too. The dog poses before a concrete water fountain on a distant, sun-soaked day, a playful grin across his lips, and for an instant, he remains the most amazing living creature on earth.

Next of Kith

Through thirty-six years as a general surgeon at New York Episcopal Hospital—during which she extracted over two thousand gallbladders, fifteen hundred appendices, scores of thyroid glands, three miles of small bowel, and eighty-four foreign bodies, including a tie clip left behind by a colleague—Dr. Emma Inkstable had grown increasingly skeptical of human weakness. Let the headshrinkers spew their claptrap about clinical depression and generalized anxiety and post-traumatic stress; in a handful of extreme cases, they might have a point. So might the social workers with their tragic tales of stolen childhoods. Yet as far as Inkstable was concerned, all that most able-bodied people required to keep themselves on track was a strong work ethic—and, failing that, an equally strong kick in the pants. If she—the homely daughter of an unmarried switchboard operator—could hold her own against the good old boys in the OR, she didn't see how anyone else had a right to complain.

"I make no apologies for how I see the world," she told Sarah Steinhoff, the spirited high school junior who'd come to write her biography. "I do realize I'm not going to win any popularity contests for what I'm saying. But if I sound callous, even heartless, it's because anybody who's lived as long as I have and doesn't sound a tad heartless must have her head in the sand."

"How old *are* you, Dr. Inkstable?"

The girl appeared oblivious to her own impertinence. She was a pretty creature, pert and busty, with a mane of auburn curls. Inkstable was glad they'd sent her. When she'd volunteered for the program, which paired aspiring female journalists from broken homes with recently retired professionals, all graduates of Hunter College, she'd feared getting stuck with some mousy, spiritless child who hid from her own shadow. Instead, they'd given her Mike Wallace in a low-cut blouse.

"I'm old enough, young lady," replied Inkstable, "to remember a time when it was considered indecorous to ask a woman her age."

"And how old is that?" inquired the girl.

Inkstable grinned, in spite of herself. "Next question."

This was their third interview. On the first—the morning after the surgeon's final day at the hospital—she'd given Sarah a realtor's tour of the apartment. During the second, she'd shown photographs from her two-year stint at the National Institutes of Health. This evening, they sat in Inkstable's kitchen, the air-conditioner groaning under the July heat, adversaries united in mutual, if grudging, respect.

"So *however* old you are," said Sarah, brandishing her microphone like a stiletto, "you've obviously lived through a lot of changes during your career. What I want to ask you about next is the AIDS crisis. Specifically, what did you do to confront it?"

"I'm really not sure what you mean."

"It was the 1980s. All of these men were dying," pressed the girl. "How did you change your life to help them? For example, you could have opened up a clinic."

Although Inkstable recognized the question as absurd—no more reasonable than asking what she'd done to end the Cold War—the girl's sincerity unsettled her. She'd always thought of herself as living a life that mattered. She'd spent her days plunging blades into human flesh. She'd forestalled death. If she'd taken a pass on marriage and children—well, marriage and children weren't the whole ball of wax. But over the last several weeks, as the sixty-eight-year-old surgeon contemplated her future (and, if she took good care of herself, that future might extend another three decades), she'd experienced a subtle yet disquieting sense that she should have accomplished more. It was a new feeling for her. Not of failure, exactly, but of detachment. Now, Sarah's cross-examination exacerbated that unease.

Fortunately, before any need arose to deflect the girl's questions, the telephone sounded in the foyer. She reached it on the second ring. "Dr. Inkstable speaking."

"I'm sorry to disturb you," replied the caller in a tone genuinely apologetic. "My name's Dr. Sucram. I'm one of the medical doctors taking care of Harry Hager."

Inkstable didn't recognize the name, but that was not unusual. She fielded countless phone calls about former patients she didn't remember—though rarely at home on a Tuesday night. What seemed strangest was that the patient apparently had suffered a hemorrhagic stroke. Hardly a matter for a general surgeon.

"I think there's some misunderstanding," interrupted Inkstable. "Are you sure you want Dr. Inkstable from *general* surgery?"

"Oh, you're a doctor," said the caller, obviously surprised. "Sorry, Mrs. Inkstable—I mean Dr. Inkstable. I didn't know. You have to understand that Mr. Hager isn't lucid at the moment. But he had a note in his wallet with your name and phone number, so the attending asked me to call you."

A glimmer of insight kindled in Inkstable's mind. Maybe Harry Hager was mustached "*Mr.* Hager" from apartment 2B. Of course! She'd seen the name on his mailbox thousands of times over the years. But while she'd always been friendly with her neighbor—he'd worked at a library, she believed—their conversations had been largely confined to small talk in the elevator and laundry room. Hager had always impressed her as being an extremely private man, as someone nourishing a rich inner life. How strange that he'd have her name and number on his person.

"Which hospital are you calling from?" she asked.

Inkstable jotted down the floor and room number. Under the circumstances, the least she could do was to pay a visit.

When she glanced up from her pad, she found the young journalist spying on her from the kitchen doorway. "Do you want to make a sick call?" Inkstable asked. She didn't have the energy to reproach the girl for eavesdropping.

Forty-five minutes later, they rode the elevator to the neurological ICU at Manhattan County Hospital. They'd caught the public bus—since her retirement, Inkstable was trying to take fewer cabs—and the surgeon enjoyed thinking that other passengers might mistake the girl for her daughter. As she'd informed Sarah en route, the care delivered at "County" was "slightly better than at a veterinary clinic." Her companion had dutifully scribbled the remark in her notebook.

On the seventh floor, the air smelled pungently of disinfectant. Fluorescent tubes cast a hideous pink glow over the tiles. At the entrance to the NICU, a double-sided yellow sign warned that the floor was wet.

"Does it feel strange?" asked the girl—following Inkstable past the nursing station. "To be in the hospital now that you're retired?"

"Not really," lied Inkstable. "In the OR, maybe I'd feel different."

They arrived at the curtained alcove where Harry Hager lay attached to a ventilator and a wall of monitors. You didn't need a medical degree, reflected Inkstable, to realize that things looked dire. Her neighbor had always been on the lean side—wiry, with delicate features—but in his hospital gown, he appeared downright scrawny. The secret truth was that she'd once thought him handsome, albeit in passing. He'd only been three years older than her, she learned from his wristband, although she'd always suspected that a solid decade stood between them. For the first time, it struck her that taking a high school student to see a dying stranger might require parental permission.

She clasped Hager's blood-mottled hand; on instinct, she felt for his pulse.

"What are his chances?" asked Sarah, cool as ice.

"We all have the same chances in the long run," quipped Inkstable—a remark honed on years of junior surgeons.

"And in the short run?"

"That," replied Inkstable cautiously, "is a question for a neurologist."

The neurologist arrived several minutes later. A second-year neurology resident, Dr. Sucram, to be precise. Behind her, looking rather like an injured lamb, stood the intern, Dr. Borrelli. "Are you Dr. Inkstable?" Sucram asked, offering up a hand with five burgundy fingernails. "I believe we spoke on the phone."

"Indeed," said Dr. Inkstable. "I take it things are as grim as they look."

Her comment seemed to fluster the resident. "I can't tell you how glad we are that you're here," she finally said. "We have to make a decision about surgery. His best bet is to put in a coil and drain some of that fluid—but, as I'm sure you know, he might come out of the OR pretty damaged. So the alternative is to let nature take its course."

A long silence ensued, punctuated only by the rhythmic bleats of the cardiac monitor and the angrier tones of the IV pump as the saline solution ran low. Suddenly, Inkstable realized that they wanted *her* to decide.

"I'm not a relative," she explained quickly. "I'm just a neighbor."

"Do you know how to get in touch with his family?"

The short answer was no. She didn't even know if he had family.

"In that case," said Dr. Sucram, "as a neighbor who knows him better than we do, you're allowed to act as his surrogate. If you're willing, that is."

"And if I'm not willing?" asked Inkstable.

Dr. Sucram toyed nervously with her engagement ring. "It would be really helpful if you could make a decision," she said. "You did know him, after all."

"What you mean," replied Inkstable, unwilling to brook nonsense, "is that you don't want to call the attending at home to tell him you can't find a relative."

That caught the junior physician off guard. Sucram shifted her weight from her right leg to her left, and for a moment Inkstable feared the young woman might flee in panic. It was July, after all, probably the resident's very first night as the ranking house officer on call. Inkstable immediately regretted her harsh words—and especially uttering them in front of the high school journalist.

If she'd been in her neighbor's shoes, Inkstable knew, she'd never have wanted the surgery. Better to end up dead than half-head—locked away in some nursing facility weaving baskets and relearning how to count. But just because those were her wishes didn't mean they were Harry Hager's. What if a relative showed up and said he'd have wanted every heroic measure?

"Okay, I'll decide. *For now*. Until you can locate his family," she said. "You'd better put in that coil and drain what you can."

⤛⫸•⫷⤜

Inkstable left her cell number with the resident—"in case of inopportune developments"—and returned to her apartment. The next morning, at the start of visiting hours, she was back at Hager's bedside. Sarah Steinhoff had secured permission from her summer program to accompany her. "It will be good exposure for her," the girl's aunt told Inkstable on the phone. "Maybe it will convince her to go into medicine like her grandfather." While the surgeon suspected that the opposite might prove true—that a day beside a stroke victim could permanently kill any thoughts of a medical career—she didn't have an ax to grind either way. She wasn't even sure why she'd come to the hospital herself, seeing as she had no formal connection to Hager. The poor man remained unconscious, his head now wrapped in gauze.

Sarah continued the interview during their visit: *What was the worst mistake you'd ever made in the operating room? How do you feel about caps on malpractice lawsuits? What had you done to advance the cause of women in surgery?* To this last question, she wanted to answer: "I existed." Instead, she humored the girl with twaddle about all of the junior colleagues she'd mentored. Meanwhile, Harry's rib cage rose and fell with his breath, his eyes swollen beneath closed lids, the cloak of impending death draped over his emaciated body.

Dr. Pastarnack, the neurology attending, made an appearance in the early afternoon. He was a pudgy, egg-bald gnome of a man; his lavender bowtie matched the handkerchief in his breast pocket. "So you're the next of kith, I hear."

"Excuse me?"

"When we can't find a patient's next of *kin*," explained Pastarnack, beaming, "I like to say that at least we've found the next of *kith*."

I'm not even that, thought Inkstable—but it wasn't worth explaining.

"Mr. Hager," called the neurologist. He rubbed the patient's sternum, yanked open an eyelid, pressed his reflex hammer against the man's nail beds. "Earth to Harry. Earth to Harry." Inkstable's neighbor remained unresponsive. Pastarnack turned to her and said, "I just looked at the imaging. That bleed did quite a number on his noggin, but we probably won't know too much for a few days yet." Then Pastarnack scanned the vitals clipboard at the foot of the bed and waved goodbye with a high-pitched "toodle-oo" that might either have been earnest or ironic.

"Sarah, dear," said Inkstable, as soon as he'd departed. "Do me a favor. If you ever become a physician and, for some inexplicable reason, you're tempted to refer to a stroke victim's brain as his 'noggin,' or to call a surrogate 'the next of kith,' kindly resign your medical license at once."

That led to a long discussion on the decline of formality in doctor-patient relationships, and in society more generally. "When I flew to my first medical conference," recalled Inkstable, "I dressed up for the plane flight. I even wore jewelry. Nowadays, people travel first-class in dungarees and T-shirts. They go *to the theater* in dungarees and T-shirts. I'll never get used to that." To Inkstable's amusement, her "biographer" embraced the other side of the argument. They were still debating the subject with gusto, two hours later, when Harry Hager blinked himself awake.

-◄◄◄•►►►-

At eight o'clock the next day, Inkstable found Zyke, her Latvian doorman, and described what had happened to Hager. Unfortunately, the box beside her neighbor's name on the building's "emergency contact" list stood blank. (Inkstable was jarred to realize that her own emergency contact, a childhood friend, had been dead for five years.) After several lengthy conversations with the building agent, which also involved input from the management company's attorneys, Zyke used a spare key to let her into Hager's apartment.

Apartment 2B was the mirror image of her own 2G. Its contents were largely as she might have anticipated: a living room lined floor to ceiling with hardcover books, a bedroom as sterile as a hotel suite. The only surprise was a peculiar musical instrument—Inkstable believed it to be an English horn—resting on the nightstand. She couldn't recall her neighbor ever playing; she'd certainly have heard him practicing from across the courtyard. No television, no photographs. More significant for Inkstable's purposes was the absence of an address book that might contain contact information regarding Hager's family. As close as she came was a Post-it note on the refrigerator that read "Cousins in Israel," followed by an international number, but she phoned multiple times and reached only a machine. Eventually, she left the name and number of the hospital. Without even the cousins' names to go on, what more could she do? Under Zyke's watchful gaze, she also packed an overnight bag with her neighbor's clothes.

Over the ensuing days, Hager displayed flickers of recovery. He managed to sit up in bed and even to swallow the Jell-O that Inkstable fed him, although he remained delirious throughout and kept mistaking the surgeon for his grandmother. He had a vague notion that he was in a hospital—but couldn't remember its name, despite daily reminders from Drs. Sucram and Borrelli. To Inkstable's surprise, the budding journalist continued to join her at Hager's bedside. "I want to see you in action," explained the girl. "In *New Yorker* profiles, the reporters follow people around." That drew an authentic laugh from the surgeon—her first laugh, she realized, since retirement.

The only unpleasant aspect of Inkstable's duties—and that was how she thought of them—was the fifteen minutes each afternoon when Dr. Pastarnack stopped by to check on his patient's progress. "So the next of kith is still with us," he declared, as though the witticism were falling on virgin ears. "And how's Harry's 'noggin' doing?" He'd close each visit by pressing the stroke victim for some absurd task: *Are you up for translating some Sanskrit today, Harry?* Or *Ready for some differential equations this morning?* Or *If you name the Roman emperors in order, Mr. Hager, I might just let you go home. . . .* Inkstable's neighbor responded with a benighted smile. Occasionally, he added a "thank you," if he concluded that gratitude was in order. As soon as Pastarnack left, Inkstable threatened that she'd report him to the state licensing authorities.

A lesser inconvenience of her newfound duties was that they required the surgeon to postpone several ventures she'd set up to launch her retirement. She'd previously committed to teaching scientific literacy in a GED program and to recording mental health journals for distribution to vision-impaired psychotherapists. Both of these endeavors, she postponed until September. She also put off a long-planned trip to Seattle, where her college roommate had settled, pleading "an illness in the family."

Would she have gone to these lengths for a different neighbor? Possibly not. The truth was that during her long hours at Hager's bedside, and especially during the bus trips to and from the hospital, Dr. Inkstable replayed her encounters with the man—numerous, seemingly trivial interactions—and she concluded that the poor fellow had been (as her own dear mother might have said) sweet on her. One time—she'd nearly forgotten—she'd run into him in the lobby, returning from her fiftieth birthday party, her canvas bag brimming over with presents; he'd congratulated her—and then knocked on her door several minutes later with a present of his own: a biography of the pioneering surgeon William Stewart Halsted. She'd never actually read the book, although she'd told him, on their next encounter, that she'd enjoyed it very much. On another occasion, only a few years ago, he'd received a crate of oranges from Haifa, and he'd invited her to claim as many as she wanted. Again, she never followed up.

At the time, it hadn't even crossed her mind that his conduct was more than neighborly—she was an old maid, after all, and not pretty—but now that they'd found her name in his wallet, she saw how oblivious she'd been. Not that she had any real regrets. What interest did she have in romantic notions of self-pity? Rather, she was simply disappointed in her own blindness.

"You used to have a crush on him, didn't you?" asked the girl.

That was five days after Hager regained consciousness; they were chatting in the visitors' lounge, waiting for him to return from an MRI. The only other occupants were a pair of obese sisters glued to a telenovela.

"Don't be foolish."

"I knew it. You're blushing," gloated Sarah. "I have very good intuition about these sorts of things."

"Well, in this case, your intuition is dead wrong," said Inkstable. "I don't believe I exchanged more than one hundred words with Harry Hager in my entire adult life."

"Maybe so. But that doesn't mean you didn't have the hots for him."

Inkstable glanced across the room, afraid the sisters might overhear her. "Enough of this nonsense already," she warned. "It doesn't matter anyway."

"It could," replied the girl. "What if he gets better? I know the odds are low, but if Mr. Hager made a full recovery, would you go out with him?"

"If grandmother had testicles," said Inkstable, "she'd be grandfather."

"What?"

"Nothing. Just an expression I shouldn't have used. But the point is the same: Harry's not going to recover, and I'm far too old to be dating anyway."

"But that's not true. My aunt's mother-in-law got remarried at eighty—"

Inkstable held up her hand. "She's her. I'm me," she said. "New topic."

And yet, from that moment forward, the remote possibility that Harry Hager might make a full recovery, and that she might "go out" with him, was never far removed from her thoughts.

-⟨⟨⟨◆⟩⟩⟩-

Hager's condition improved at a glacial pace. He had good moments, when he seemed to recognize Inkstable, and one breakthrough, when he remembered her name was Emma, but ten minutes later, he was calling her Granny Louise and asking her for help with his schoolwork. Yet cognitive reconstitution after a stroke, Inkstable recognized, often took many months. Even years. She'd read somewhere about a firefighter in Iowa or Idaho who'd awoken from a post-hemorrhage coma after three *decades*. Compared to that hapless fellow, Harry seemed in strong shape. By the end of his second week in the hospital, he'd been transferred to a general neurology unit and she'd somehow managed to get him into his own clothes.

"Thank you kindly," he said, admiring his new look in her pocket mirror. "I'm not sure who you are, but I do appreciate your assistance."

Even in his impaired state, one sensed her neighbor to be a gentle soul—in many ways, the spitting opposite of Inkstable. Since his stroke, he'd sprouted a fine white beard to match his mustache. Much of the bruising around his nose and chin had resolved. Once he'd traded in his hospital gown for a collared shirt, he managed to throw the cloak of death off his frame. Now she could not deny the truth: Harry Hager was indeed a strikingly handsome man.

"And who is this young lady?" he asked, smiling at the girl.

"I'm Sarah," she said.

"Are you my daughter?" asked Hager.

Sarah smiled. "I'm not. I'm just a friend."

"Are you *her* daughter?" he asked again, glancing at the surgeon.

"I'm nobody's daughter," said Sarah. "I'm a friend of Dr. Inkstable."

The girl's answer upset Inkstable—unreasonably so. She found herself wishing that Sarah had lied. Why not claim she was her daughter? In fact, why not say she was her daughter *and* Hager's daughter? It was fantastical nonsense, she understood, but wasn't everyone entitled to a small dose of fantastical nonsense?

"I'm glad you're here anyway," said Hager. "If I did have a daughter, I'm sure I'd want her to be like you."

Later that day, when Sarah left for a dental checkup, Inkstable found herself alone with Hager for the first time since he'd regained consciousness. She held a straw to his lips, helping him drink a boxed juice. His right arm remained entirely paralyzed and he still had difficulty manipulating the fingers in his left hand. "It looks like it's just the two of us this afternoon," she said.

"I'm grateful for the company."

"Do you remember who I am?" she asked.

He stared at her blankly. "I'm sorry. I'm afraid I don't."

"It's Emma. Emma Inkstable. From across the courtyard," she said. "You carried my name around in your wallet."

"I'm sure I did," he agreed. "If you say so."

"Try to remember, Harry. *Please.* You gave me a biography of William Steward Halsted for my fiftieth birthday . . . and one time, you received a crate of oranges from your cousins in Haifa and you invited me to share them."

"That's right. My cousins," he said.

"So you do remember?"

"I don't know," he replied. "I think I might have cousins in Israel. But if I'm mistaken, please don't be angry at me."

"Nobody's going to be angry at you, Harry." She felt her frustration mounting, the urge to shake him like a broken vending machine until coins fell out. "I'm just trying to jog your memory." She took a deep breath and added, "You had a crush on me once. We were going to go out together . . . like a couple."

"Were we?"

"Yes, we were," she answered decisively. "But we'll have plenty of time to talk about that later. Once you've regained your strength."

They were interrupted an instant later by the shift nurse, performing her afternoon temperature check. Her presence reminded Inkstable of how different it felt to be a visitor. On surgery rounds, she'd have asked the nurse to return once she'd left. When they were alone again, Inkstable asked, "Do you play the English horn?"

"I don't know," answered Hager. "Do I?"

Inkstable regretted not having brought the instrument with her. She'd seen videos of amnesiacs playing Chopin and Tchaikovsky on the piano. Mightn't Hager pipe out a sonata or two on the English horn? She even considered asking Zyke for the spare key to Hager's apartment again—but realistically, she knew, they'd have little patience for brass performances on the neurology ward. Besides, when she'd mentioned the instrument the next morning, he had absolutely no memory of their conversation.

⸙

She knew what was coming, even before the nitwit Pastarnack asked to speak with her alone in the corridor. He'd traded in his bowtie for what looked like an honest-to-god ascot and he sported a peculiar silk scarf around his neck. "I hate to be the one to tell you this," he explained, "but I spent all morning on the phone with the insurance company. Alas, your kith has to depart."

"All morning," echoed Inkstable. "Really."

"You'll have to talk to the social worker about your options. Quite frankly, I don't see him getting much out of sub-acute rehab. It's either home with services or a skilled nursing facility—but I'll leave that for you to sort out."

"How thoughtful of you."

"In any case," said the neurologist, "Harry's fortunate to have you. Strong family—or nonfamily, as the case may be—support is the most important factor in a patient's long-term prognosis."

This was too much for Inkstable. "Do you really believe that, Dr. Pastarnack? More important than the extent of tissue damage? So a patient with a massive mid-cerebral bleed and a loyal wife is better off than a loner with a tiny infarct? In my day, they taught that social support was valuable—but rarely determinant."

The look of sheer bewilderment on the neurologist's face brought Inkstable a surge of pleasure, the same joy she'd always felt making fast-paced decisions in the OR. Unwilling to sacrifice even an ounce of her satisfaction, she turned on her heels and abandoned Pastarnack before he had a chance to respond. But, nitwit that he was, he'd been correct in one regard: Harry was lucky to have her.

She consulted with the social worker early the following morning, Sarah Steinhoff joining them in what was almost a "family" meeting. It turned out that Hager had been a patient at County once before, for a hernia repair, and so they had all of his records—including details on his supplemental insurance. He'd been a planner. Thanks to multiple, over-lapping policies, he'd have a strong claim for twenty-four-hour nursing care. (Inkstable couldn't help wondering about her own insurance arrange-ments, which she doubted were nearly so generous.) By the end of the day, they'd arranged for Hager to return to his apartment. "It makes the most sense," she assured the social worker. "This way I can visit him every day—even more often, if necessary. And maybe the familiar settings will jog his memory."

"I do hope so," agreed the social worker. She filled out a series of computerized forms while they spoke. At one question, she asked, "And you are his . . . ?"

"Girlfriend," Inkstable declared.

Sarah threw her a puzzled look—to which she responded with a stern glare.

Once they'd left the social worker's office, she said, "It's easier this way. What does it matter if they write "girlfriend" on some pointless form anyway?"

"You don't need to sound so defensive," answered the girl, smirking. "If you want to be Harry's girlfriend, who am I to disagree?"

"Impertinent little fiend," said Inkstable. "That's what you are, young lady. An impertinent little fiend." But that didn't stop her from taking the girl out for pizza.

-◄◄◄◆►►►-

The Israeli cousins, Bonnie and Albert, arrived while Inkstable and the budding journalist were out. When Inkstable returned to the neurology ward, she found the wife in a heated discussion with the social worker. The pair were standing at the foot of Harry's bed. Albert, who looked to be in his seventies—considerably older than his wife—sat by the window, reading the *Wall Street Journal.* "Am I interrupting?" inquired the surgeon.

"Not at all," replied the social worker. "I was just explaining to Mrs. Nalaskowski the arrangements we've made." She lowered her voice—although it was unclear who could possibly overhear. "There seems to be some disagreement."

"Bonnie. Harry's cousin," said the newcomer, extending a hand. She spoke with a faint accent. "His uncle was my father. And you are?"

"Emma Inkstable," answered the surgeon. She was tempted to add, "his girlfriend," but she didn't dare. "I live in his building."

"You're the neighbor who phoned us, aren't you? I'm sorry it took so long to get here. We spend our winters in Maine. They're supposed to forward our calls, but. . . . " She shrugged. "You know how it is."

"I should excuse myself," interjected the social worker.

"Please don't," objected Bonnie. "I'd like to get this all sorted out quickly."

Inkstable detected menace in the cousin's tone. Behind her, Sarah Steinhoff was dutifully scribbling notes in her journal. "What's to sort out?" asked the surgeon.

"We're planning on taking Harry back to Israel with us," said the cousin. "This week. We've arranged for a place in the same nursing home with my parents."

"But I've already set up round-the-clock care," insisted Inkstable. "I realize you have the best of intentions, but I'm confident Harry would have wanted to stay here."

The woman stood arms akimbo, her eyes fierce under heavy liner. "Who are you to tell me what Harry would want?" She looked to the social worker for support. "My understanding was that family has the final say."

"I'm afraid she's right, Dr. Inkstable. They are cousins."

"And what am I?" demanded the surgeon.

Yet she already knew the answer. Nothing. To Harry Hager, legally speaking, she was no more than a hunk of stone. If she'd had a scalpel at that instant, she had little doubt she'd have carved open the Israeli cousin's chest.

"I appreciate your efforts," said the woman—in a voice more hostile than conciliatory. "But family is family. Surely, you understand."

Inkstable remained inside her own apartment for the next several days, knowing that movers were likely at work across the corridor. Those floor-to-ceiling bookshelves would need to be emptied from her neighbor's apartment; everything—even that strange brass instrument—would have to go, all of the poor man's earthly goods sold on E-bay or donated to charity or discarded. To distract herself, the surgeon rifled through her own closet until she uncovered Robustelli's biography of Halsted, which had gathered years of dust atop a box of bird-watching guides. It was a fascinating read and a well-earned diversion. By the end of the week, she'd managed to recognize her relationship with Harry Hager for what it had been: a pipe dream. For all she knew, he'd had her name in his wallet because he wanted to complain about noise from across the courtyard or to solicit her vote for the co-op board. Who could ever know? And if she wanted to "go out" with someone—which seemed rather silly at her age— she could do a lot better than a cognitively impaired stroke survivor. On Friday afternoon, she checked with Zyke and was relieved to learn that

Harry's cousins had cleared out his apartment. Even the name "H. Hager" had been stripped from his mailbox in the vestibule, leaving behind only a pale band of discolored metal.

Inkstable was feeling ready to relaunch her retirement—to put this unfortunate interruption behind her—when the doorbell rang, shortly before noon on Saturday. She answered the door in her bathrobe, expecting a delivery. Instead, the young journalist stood at the threshold. The girl sported a backwards baseball cap and a spaghetti-strap top that exposed far too much midriff. In spite of that, Inkstable was delighted to see her. To the girl's surprise, Inkstable offered her a hug.

"To what do I owe this honor?" asked the surgeon.

"I finished my biography," replied Sarah—holding out a report binder. "I thought you'd want to read it before I turn it in."

She'd almost forgotten about the writing project. She flipped through the crisp, white pages. The girl had obviously put in a great deal of effort.

"I thought maybe you'd read it while I'm here," said Sarah. "It's not that long."

"I guess I can," agreed Inkstable. "Why don't you come into the kitchen and I'll get you a nice glass of milk. And would you like some fruit? I have fresh cantaloupe."

Only when the girl was finally settled at the table with a slice of melon and a bowl of white grapes did the surgeon open the manuscript. The title page read:

DR. EMMA ESMERALDA INKSTABLE: A POSSIBLE LIFE

BY

SARAH LAUREN STEINHOFF

She turned the page and entered the world of her own childhood: the years spent in the railroad apartment above the cobbler shop, where the air always stank of rotting leather; her mother's death from esophageal cancer; the scholarships that gave her enough of a financial foundation to work her way through Hunter and Yale Med. She was about to compliment the young journalist on her cogent, colorful prose style, when on page seventeen, she found herself meeting Harry Hager in the elevator. It was Christmas Eve, and she'd had a smidgen too much eggnog at the departmental holiday party. When her heel broke—*she didn't even wear heels!*—and she twisted her ankle, the librarian helped her back to her apartment. By the following week, they were an item.

She skimmed through the pages that followed. She saw the words "wedding," "anniversary," "children." Each blow hit her in the chest like artillery and her entire body started to tremble.

"What have you done?" the surgeon demanded. "What *have* you done?"

A look of alarm swallowed the girl's features. "I didn't mean to get you upset, Dr. Inkstable. Honestly, I didn't," she said. "I was just trying to be creative. . . and it has a happy ending. I thought you'd like it this way."

And then the girl was sobbing, and Inkstable was sobbing, and somewhere, far away, a stranger was blowing the first joyful notes on her newly acquired English horn.

Right of Way

-‹‹‹◆›››-

What to call the street where I grew up—a nondescript six blocks of one-way asphalt connecting Van Buren Avenue to Burlingame Parkway—never troubled us until the spring of my thirteenth birthday, when somebody pilfered all twelve signs that identified the thoroughfare as Rabbit Meadow Lane. These signs, identical cast-aluminum fixtures attached to their posts with screws and washers, dated from the early 1950s, and they vanished on the same foggy Sunday night in April, leaving in their wake the orphaned tags belonging to the intersecting cross streets. Why our bandit hadn't pinched these signs as well remained a mystery—as did why someone would want twelve identical street signs in the first place—but the resulting conflict pitted neighbor against neighbor and undermined the quiet civility that had long reigned over our upper-middle-class corner of Creve Coeur.

I don't mean to suggest that the inhabitants of Rabbit Meadow Lane had ever formed a tight-knit community. We did not. But the physicians and university professors and insurance executives—like my own father—who'd revitalized the patchwork of blocks behind the municipal courthouse in the 1980s, transforming rundown tenements into refurbished town-houses, belonged to that dying breed of Rockefeller Republicans who pruned their own hedges, kept their sidewalks free from ice, hand-delivered misdirected mail promptly, and minded their own damn business. They'd created "a suburb within a city," my father boasted—and during his three terms representing our district on the Board of Aldermen, he sponsored legislation to create an independent "Village of Rabbit Meadow" beyond Creve Coeur's taxation authority. That may explain my old man's outrage when, shortly after the Great Sign Robbery, a librarian named Bernard Pozner circulated a petition to change the name of our street.

"Leo Lippitt isn't going to look the other way," warned my father at breakfast one Sunday, referring to himself in the third person—a sure indication that he was upset. "So there aren't any rabbits. It's not like we're advertising a pet store. Tell me, Ellen. Is there still a wall on Wall Street?"

My mother continued feeding Gerber apple puree to my baby sister. "It *is* kind of funny, you know. We've lived here how many years? And never once did I pause to ask, Why is our street named after rabbits, if there aren't any?"

"Jesus, Ellen. Whose side are you on?"

"I suppose there must have been rabbits once," mused my mother. "When do you think the rabbits last lived here?"

"How the hell should I know?" My father pushed his chair away from the table and paced across the linoleum. "I could be more sympathetic if the name were offensive or confusing—if it belonged to a colonial slave trader . . . or if we lived on Jefferson Davis Terrace. Although changing would *still* be inconvenient. But rabbits? Leo Lippitt isn't going to let himself be branded a racist for defending rabbits."

Pozner apparently hoped to rename the street after Algernon McFlythe, an African American poet who'd been born at #15 before World War I. The librarian had been going door to door, claiming the missing signs offered the perfect opportunity for "progress," and distributing mimeographed samples of McFlythe's verse.

"I tell you what, Ellen," said my father, "Joshua and his dad are going to pay a visit to the Pozner residence this morning. What do you say to that, Joshua? Are you ready to stand up for Rabbit Meadow?"

"I don't feel well," I lied. "My head hurts."

Bernard Pozner's daughter, Priscilla, was two grades ahead of me at Hutchinson High School—a weird, tomboyish creature whom I dreamed of marrying. The last thing on earth I wanted was to show up at her house with my father.

"Nothing cures a headache like fresh air. Unless you have a brain tumor." My old man winked at me. Then he retrieved his sweater from the hook behind the door. I secretly hoped that I would contract a brain tumor—at least, a benign one—just to serve him right. "Anyway, it's not as though McFlythe lives here anymore either, no more than the rabbits do. I read some of his poems, by the way. Very bleak stuff. I tried to keep an open mind, but the truth is I found them rather tedious."

"Please don't cause trouble, Leo," admonished my mother. "If you die of a heart attack, nobody will care what the street is called."

"Nobody's causing trouble. We're just paying a neighborly visit," said my father. "Now if your son would stop lollygagging and help clear the table. . . ."

⋘◆⋙

Although the Pozners lived only six blocks away—at the very base of our street, just off the corner from Van Buren—my father preferred to cover the short distance at the wheel of his Buick. He was a skilled driver, but an aggressive one, especially when angry, and he rolled through each of the four-way stops. Twice, he cut off vehicles from the cross streets as they sought to exercise the right-of-way. By the time we pulled up to the Pozners' residence ten minutes later—a tidy brick structure with geranium boxes tucked below the dormer windows—I'd grown carsick and pale with terror.

We passed through the wrought-iron swinging gate. My father placed his hand on my shoulder and observed, "Always meet your adversary face to face. One of the most valuable lessons I've learned in life is that a pair of reasonable men can resolve almost any disagreement with twenty minutes of honest conversation." He grinned and added, "Women, I'm afraid, are another matter entirely." Then he pressed the buzzer, and in a moment, we stood face to face with Bernard Pozner.

The librarian turned out to be a short, slight-framed man with a chevron moustache who looked a generation older than my parents. After my father introduced us, referring to me as his "progeny," Pozner led the way into a cluttered parlor off the foyer. Commemorative posters covered every inch of wall space, honoring Harriet Tubman and the Scottsboro Boys and the National American Woman Suffrage Association. A picket sign, resting against the coffee table, demanded an immediate nuclear freeze. Atop the baby grand piano, assorted photographs depicted a heavy-set, soft-featured woman whom I later discovered to be the librarian's late wife—Priscilla's dead mother—killed ten years earlier in a collision at a railroad crossing. Mercifully, there was no trace of Priscilla herself. Pozner steered us toward a damask sofa and settled into a matching armchair.

Twenty minutes of honest conversation did little to resolve the dispute. "So I hear you're troubled by the name of our street," began my father, sounding reasonable enough, but soon he was lecturing Pozner on the financial consequences of historical revisionism. "Have you considered how many small businesses will have to reprint their stationery? You'll be taking money directly out of the pockets of every dentist and accountant with a home office." That led Bernard Pozner to remark that the owners of F. W. Woolworth had worried about the economic backlash from desegregating lunch counters, and soon enough, the two men were arguing past each other in raised voices. Eventually, I slipped away on the pretext of visiting the bathroom.

My actual goal was to search the Pozner residence for hidden passages. During eighth grade, awkward and friendless, I'd read about the secret tunnels constructed by Tsar Paul I at Mikhailovsky Castle, and about the concealed vaults layered within Egyptian pyramids, and I longed to discover similar chambers in Creve Coeur that might prove an antidote to the relentless boredom of weekend afternoons. In some of my fantasies, these passageways led to pirate loot. In others, to kidnapped teenage girls awaiting rescue. That I could possibly believe such treasures lurked behind the cedar paneling inside our neighbors' cupboards stands as a testament to my own desperation, but while my father denounced Algernon McFlythe as a third-rate poet, I tapped my fingers along the wainscoting, listening for a hollow reply. No luck. Then I climbed to the second story landing and explored the adjacent walk-in closets where the Pozners stored china and linen. I lit a match inside the crawlspace to expose a draft—as I'd seen a British spy once do on television. A year of snooping had turned me into an old pro. Sadly, the Pozners' walls proved unyielding.

A methodical search should have made my next stop the attic: every schoolboy learns that attics, cellars, and closets conceal the vast share of fake paneling, rivaled only by the portraits hanging above fireplace mantels. Yet the route to the attic stairs led past the open door of Priscilla's bedroom. On impulse—in what was, for a serious detective, a burst of unforgivable adolescent weakness—I poked my head inside.

I'd visited girls' bedrooms before, although my experience was limited to those of my twin cousins in Pontefract and the older daughters of my parents' various childhood friends. I'd also seen countless female bedrooms on television. Those rooms all contained fluffy pink pillows atop fluffy white bedding, chambers often decorated with posters of popular actors and bands. None of that prepared me for the stark, somber aura that enveloped every inch of Priscilla's personal space. She slept on black bedding. She had draped black throw cloths over the nightstands. Her pillows, rather than pink and fluffy, were shaded the darkest maroon, and instead of tributes to movie stars and musicians, the walls displayed an odd assortment of street maps: Downtown St. Louis; North and South Dakota; hiking trails of Yosemite. Some bore the logo of the American Automobile Association; others appeared torn from a Rand McNally road atlas. My desire for Priscilla Pozner rose exponentially.

"Caught you!"

I spun around just as Priscilla switched on the overhead light. She stood in the entryway, her fists braced against her fleshy hips. I'd never actually spoken to her before at school, but I knew she recognized me, and my temples swelled with blood.

"What are you doing in here?" she demanded.

"Nothing." I sensed the tears welling behind my eyes. "Honest."

"Bullshit. You were going to spy on me, weren't you? Confess and I'll go easy on you." Priscilla stepped into the room; she was smirking. "Spit it out. You planned to hide under the bed or in the closet so you could watch me get naked."

The word "naked" propelled even more blood into my forehead. I found my eyes focused on the buckles of Priscilla's boots. "I swear I wasn't spying," I stammered—and unable to fashion a plausible lie, I resorted to a full confession. "I know you're going to laugh at me," I said. "I was searching for a secret passage."

"Oh my God. For real?"

I nodded—still unable to make eye contact. "Pathetic, isn't it?"

She didn't have an opportunity to agree. At that instant, my father's voice rattled the Pozners' masonry. "Joshua! Get your ass down here," he shouted. "You can use the goddamn toilet at our house."

I raced past Priscilla and darted down the stairs. She followed.

My father stood in the foyer, alone, veins pulsating in his neck. "Where the hell have you been?" he cried. "I was afraid you'd fallen in."

Priscilla laughed at his remark. I bolted out the front door and through the iron gate, stopping only when I'd reached the safety of the Buick.

-⟨⟨⟨◆⟩⟩⟩-

My father used the drive home as a teachable moment. "Do you know what the word 'overweening' means, Joshua?" he asked—and then he proceeded to use it in multiple sentences about Bernard Pozner. "Or maybe, since I am a racist, after all, I should define it in racial terms," he said. "Here's a good SAT analogy for you. *Uppity is to Negro as Overweening is to Caucasian.*" Apparently, the librarian had indeed insinuated that my father was a bigot—which my old man took as a license for off-color humor. He cruised through the stop signs again, but I hardly noticed. Now that I'd humiliated myself in front of Priscilla, I welcomed a broadside collision. The following morning, for the first and only time in my memory, I feigned illness to avoid school. I even induced a bout of vomiting to allay my mother's suspicions, offering her a firsthand peek at my half-digested supper. Sticking a toothbrush down my throat seemed far preferable to encountering Priscilla in the cafeteria.

I was lounging in bed, staring aimlessly as the ceiling, when the doorbell rang later that afternoon. To my surprise, my mother summoned me downstairs—and Priscilla Pozner herself was waiting in our vestibule. She sported a fashionably torn T-shirt above a pair of cargo pants. Mom flashed me a smile and disappeared into the kitchen. Suddenly, I found myself alone with the most tantalizing being I'd ever met.

"I've got something to show you," she said.

She retreated out the door and I followed. Why, precisely, I found Priscilla so alluring remains a puzzle—even to my adult self. She wasn't particularly pretty, certainly not compared to Lauren Paderewski or long-legged Maria Arcaya. Dating her didn't promise to make me more popular. I also couldn't attribute my attraction to any display of interest or generosity she'd shown toward me. Before our encounter in her bedroom, she'd never even acknowledged my existence. And yet something about her—not merely her peculiarity, but her brazen confidence in her own peculiarity—made me trail her down Rabbit Meadow Lane like a blind, starving puppy.

Twilight had settled over the street. Mourning doves cooed atop the power lines; squirrels scampered across the scraps of yard around the Congregational Church. As we neared Priscilla's block, I imagined she might be leading me back to her shrouded bedroom for a night of torrid seduction. Yet when we scaled her front steps, she tiptoed into the flower beds—careful to avoid the tidy rows of marigolds and begonias—and veered around the side of the house.

A narrow slate path separated the structure from a mesh fence; golden sumac sprouted along the perimeter. Priscilla paused at the base of the chimney and retrieved a pair of industrial flashlights from a utility box. Then she led us to the far corner of the house, where an ailanthus tree leaned against the brickwork. Beneath the tree, at a forty-five-degree angle, lay a pair of raised doors—what looked like the entrance to a storm cellar, at least to a boy whose only knowledge of storm cellars came from *The Wizard of Oz*. Not since we'd left my house had Priscilla uttered a word.

She handed me a flashlight and I climbed through the double doors. If her goal had been to murder me, I realize, I couldn't have made the task any easier.

The temperature inside the cellar sent gooseflesh down my bare arms; the air smelled vaguely of mildew. I panned the flashlight into the darkness, expecting to find myself inside a confined space, possibly one lined with crates of canned soup. But the chamber proved enormous—the size of our high school gymnasium. I didn't see any packaged food or furniture, at least not nearby, just a few scattered milk crates and a toolbox. And then I noticed the signs laid out along the concrete like tombstones: twelve aluminum tags announcing "Rabbit Meadow Lane." There were other signs, too: "Hours – Creve Coeur Public Library" and "Hager Pond Visitors Center" and "Alumni Hall," the last emblazoned with the distinctive logo of Marston Moor College.

"It's a fallout shelter," said Priscilla. "For when the Russians spill coffee on their nuclear football and the world comes to an end."

I strove to take this revelation in stride. "Did your dad build this?"

"Lord, no. Some deranged old widow spent her fortune on this back in the 1950s. She was convinced the world was going to end on January 1, 1960. I have carbon copies of the batty letters she sent to politicians."

"That's wild," I said—to display interest.

"Papa knows this place exists, but he's too busy chaining himself to courthouses to remember," she added. "Now here's the kicker. That widowed nutcase never made it to 1960. She went to a rotary club picnic and choked to death on a pork chop."

Priscilla laughed—a raucous, joyful laugh tinged with venom. I wasn't exactly sure why the widow's death was so amusing, but I forced a smile.

My crush dusted off a milk crate and sat down. I followed her lead. I noticed that she'd shut the storm doors behind us, and now she turned off her flashlight, leaving my thin beam the only source of light within the chamber. Then she reached over and extinguished mine.

"I bet you want to know about the signs," said Priscilla. "Here's the deal. My dad is obsessed with making order in the world. Fixing things. Renaming goddamn streets after forgotten poets. So I'm doing my best to create some disorder. Manufactured chaos. That way, we balance out our influence."

In hindsight, her explanation begs countless questions. At the moment, Priscilla's reasoning made perfect sense. "So you steal signs," I said.

"What I like about signs is that they can say completely different things at the same time," she said. Her voice sounded louder in the darkness. "Take a yellow light. For some people, a yellow light is a warning to slow down. And for others, it's a call to accelerate. Do you see what I mean?"

"Kind of."

"But we also expect certain things of signs. They're a reminder of how predictable we are as human beings. What would you do if you were driving one day and you saw a purple stoplight? Would you slow down? Or would you accelerate?"

I didn't answer. I was still two years away from my learner's permit.

"You see my point," declared Priscilla—as though she'd unraveled a complex mathematical puzzle. "*I* want to be like a purple stoplight."

I struggled to wrap my thirteen-year-old mind around purple traffic lights, but my brain had lurched into overdrive. In less than eight hours, I'd gone from self-induced vomiting to exploring a secret underground chamber with the girl of my dreams.

"You're probably wondering why I'm showing you all this," said Priscilla.

I nodded—and then realized she couldn't see me.

"I'm ready for bigger projects," she announced. "*Two-person* projects. I've got a battery-powered metal saw, so we can start going after road signs—even highway signs—but I'll need you to help me carry them."

She laughed again. "Do you know how much chaos we could cause by collecting all the one-way signs in Creve Coeur?"

"A lot," I said.

"More than a lot," she said.

"Why aren't you afraid that I'll turn you in?"

She switched her flashlight back on. "Because I have good instincts." She stood up and led me across the fallout shelter. "You thought I'd invited you down here to kiss you, didn't you? Come on. Admit it."

"I guess."

"I knew it," she said.

And then she opened the double doors, letting any further discussion of kissing melt away in the moonlight. We said goodbye with a wave.

By the time I arrived home, my father was already seated at the dinner table with his shirtsleeves rolled to the elbows. He glanced pointedly at his wristwatch. "Look who turned up, Ellen," he said. "And you're looking healthier than I was led to believe. If we're lucky, your mother and I can still get our down payment back on that coffin."

"Please, Leo," said my mother. "Don't even joke."

I squeezed my hands together in my lap, praying he wouldn't mention Priscilla. It wasn't until my mother served dessert that I finally let down my guard. I was dipping strawberries into fresh whipped cream when my father said, "You're old enough to choose your own friends, Joshua. But a word to the wise. That Pozner girl is ugly as sin. You're not doing yourself any favors being seen with a girl like that." He nodded and pumped his fist in the air at chin level, his perennial gesture for instilling confidence in his progeny. "Trust me, Joshua. You can do better." To this day, I'm still not certain which one of us he was trying to reassure.

—⟪⟨◆⟩⟫—

The Rabbit Meadow controversy soon took a vicious turn. In an interview with the *Creve Coeur Sentinel*, my father insinuated—without naming any names—that the "agitators" who wanted to commemorate McFlythe might have orchestrated the original disappearance of the signs. In response, Bernard Pozner invited Reverend Tarwell Shuttlesworth from the Boston NAACP to hold a rally on the steps of the public library—and the minister did mention my father by name. On the following Sunday, students from Marston Moor College paraded through our neighborhood, wearing bunny ears and chanting, "Where are the rabbits?" The sole African American family on our block, the Weldons, found themselves besieged by the regional media for comment—all the more so, when it was revealed that Dr. Weldon preferred to keep the street name unchanged. Even Michael Dukakis, campaigning for the Democratic presidential nomination in nearby Tierney Falls, was asked for his opinion. To my father, whose primary life goal was to raise his family in tranquility, the attention proved infuriating. Yet the worst blow to my old man occurred when a Klan chapter from South Carolina mailed him a fan letter, prompting him to send off an indignant, seventeen-page reply.

I was concerned to see my old man growing increasingly agitated; Priscilla found the entire dispute hilarious. "You'd think they were arguing over human sacrifices," she said. "Who the fuck cares what we call this place? *Please*. In Japan, streets don't even have names."

We were camped out in the underground shelter, where we'd been meeting every few nights for the prior two weeks, plotting our chicanery. Priscilla initiated each rendezvous. I waited at home after school, hoping she'd appear in our foyer, and sometimes she did. What occupied her on the evenings that we didn't hang out together remained a mystery, and I feared that asking would make me sound too desperate for her company.

"Tonight's the night," she announced. "Isn't that fog beautiful? I could do a striptease on the sidewalk and I doubt anyone would notice." My companion sounded gleeful. "They've also set up for overnight roadwork along the parkway, so nobody should be able to hear us. It's almost too perfect."

Priscilla dropped to her knees, where a map of Creve Coeur lay spread over the concrete, and examined the street plan. She'd already marked out multiple targets with red ink. "We'll start off small," she declared. "Four signs, tops." She named the intersections where the vulnerable one-way markers awaited.

"Are you sure about this?" I asked. "What if somebody ends up driving the wrong way down one of these streets?"

"That's the whole point."

She crawled several yards into the darkness and returned with the plastic case that contained the battery-powered metal saw. "It's not a big deal, even if we get caught. I've still got another four months before I turn sixteen—so if I get arrested, it won't stay on my permanent record. They'll probably just send you home with a warning."

My age was a sore spot—and Priscilla probably realized that her dig was precisely the way to motivate me to action. Three hours later, we were seated in the exact same spot, surrounded by the truncated heads of four one-way signs. I'd sweated through my T-shirt—and I'd nearly lost control of my bladder when a distant siren erupted while Priscilla was sawing—but I'd proven myself. Or so I thought.

"Nice work," said my companion. "But you'd better run home. We can celebrate some other time."

Earlier, once we'd decided on a plan, I'd phoned my mother from Priscilla's kitchen and told her that I was going to the movies. In the background, I'd heard my father saying something about it being a school night, so I'd hung up quickly, before I'd secured approval. *It's always easier to ask for forgiveness than for permission*, Priscilla had coached me. Of course, that meant there'd be hell to pay the moment I stepped through the front door. I could already anticipate my father threatening to exile me to boarding school in New Hampshire.

Priscilla tied the storm doors shut from the outside and accompanied me to the street. "I guess you can kiss me now," she said. "If you really want to."

And I did really want to. So I pressed my lips onto hers.

Our entire interaction lasted fewer than ten seconds; I was terrified of making contact with any other part of Priscilla's body, so I drew my torso away from hers, while my head leaned inwards. I found my mind racing: Was I supposed to thank Priscilla? To tell her that I loved her? Never in my entire life had I felt as frightened of screwing up.

Priscilla didn't give me a chance to saying anything.

"If you tell anyone I kissed you," she said, "I'll claw your eyes out."

-⧼⧼◆⧽⧽-

I'd been counting on my mother to shelter me from my old man's wrath, but I arrived home to find that she'd gone to bed early, leaving a handwritten note atop the kitchen table that reminded me to set my alarm clock. My father must have heard the front door open. He called for me to join him in his study, and the volume of his voice told me that my mother wasn't actually sleeping, merely yielding us space.

I found my old man relaxing in his favorite easy chair, wearing his silk dressing gown and nursing a scotch. He appeared more weary than angry.

"I have a right to be displeased with you, Joshua. I even have a right, as your father, to prohibit you from seeing that Pozner girl," he said—as much to himself as to me. "But what good would that do? You'd only want to see her all the more . . . and I'm confident you'd succeed in doing so." He shook his head. "No, that's not the way. So why don't you sit down and we'll have healthy chat, man to man."

I settled onto the edge of the opposite armchair. I'd braced myself for a grounding, or even banishment, but I was unprepared for my father's confessional tone. That was the first time I'd ever sensed his vulnerability—and it terrified me.

"Leo Lippitt isn't a particularly brilliant man. Leo Lippitt isn't a particularly successful man," said my father. "He's not a cardiologist, like his brother. He's never going to run a large insurance firm. But that's all right. Because what Leo Lippitt *does* know is who he is—and that's far more important than being a cardiologist or chairman of the board of General Motors. Am I making sense?"

"Yes, absolutely" I agreed.

"Good. Because sometimes I wonder." He paused—as though he'd lost his train of thought. "Now, what I wanted to say was that there are two sorts of people in this world—or, at least, in places like Creve Coeur. Some men wake up each morning and think how fortunate they are to have secure jobs, and food on the table for their families, and the right to vote and speak their mind, and all that. They understand *rationally* that life isn't perfect—that society is not without its flaws—but they recognize that, on the whole, they're better off than most. And they're grateful."

My father uncapped the scotch bottle and topped off his glass. I'd never seen him drink liquor before, except when we had company.

"Other men wake up in the morning and see what's wrong with the world. They climb out of bed one morning and, on a whim, decide that a street would be better named after a dead writer than a warren of rabbits—and they turn the whole goddamn planet upside-down to make their point. Are you following me?"

"They turn the planet upside-down," I echoed.

"Exactly," said my father—as though the idea had been entirely my own. "And a girl who grows up in a home where everything is upside-down can't be expected to turn out right-side up. That's all I'm saying." My father rested his snifter on the arm of his chair. He seemed so old, at that moment, although he was only in his early forties—younger than I am today. "The reason your mother and I get along so well is that, fundamentally, we're the same sort of people. Oil mixes best with oil. It's entirely up to you whether you learn that lesson the easy way or the hard way."

I waited for him to say more, but he merely shrugged.

"Get a good night's sleep," he urged. "And remember, your parents love you."

The next morning—a Saturday—brought two unpleasant discoveries. We'd just settled down to breakfast as a family when the phone rang; my father stepped through the dining room door with the telephone, holding the console in one hand and the receiver in the other, then returned five minutes later with his eyes apoplectic.

"Do we have plans for this evening, Ellen?" he asked.

"Actually, we do. Tonight's that benefit for your aunt."

My Aunt Ida volunteered with a charity that taught quilting to female prisoners.

"We'll have to apologize and send her a check," said my father. "You'll be coming with me to the board meeting tonight. All of you. I want Shuttlesworth and his crew to see that we're a family community, not some band of racist hooligans. Can you bring the kids to City Hall around nine o'clock? Baby Jodi too."

"Since when do you meet on Saturdays?"

"Since that crackpot Pozner persuaded Chet Chapin to hold an emergency session on the subject of street names." My father returned the telephone console to its perch atop a stack of yellow pages. "Who ever heard of legislating street names? Pretty soon we'll have to vote to install a fire hydrant."

That was when I noticed the morning *Sentinel*, laid out neatly beside my father's place setting. "SIGN SNATCHER SNARLS SIDE STREETS," read the headlines. "NEAR MISS ON VAN BUREN." I skimmed the portion of the article above the fold. Fortunately, although the missing signs had led to some brief chaos, nobody had been injured. I also discovered that stealing municipal property was a Class B felony, punishable by four years in prison. My father opened the newspaper before I'd finished reading, and turned to the "Mailbag & Commentary" section. He enjoyed reading the craziest letters aloud to my mother.

"Make certain Joshua wears a tie tonight. For once, Leo Lippitt's son can look respectable," he said from behind the paper—all of last night's laxity having evaporated with the dawn. "And Ellen. Be prepared to stay late."

-‹‹‹•›››-

I mustered the courage to seek out Priscilla that morning—longing desperately to see her, but reluctant, after the tête-à-tête with my old man, to have her show up in our foyer. My hope was to meet her inside the fallout shelter, but I found the storm doors bound shut with twine. Reluctantly, I rang the Pozners' buzzer.

Bernard Pozner opened the front door. He looked surprised to see me—possibly even disappointed. "You're Priscilla's friend," he observed. From the parlor rose the murmur of simmering voices. "You'll find her upstairs," he instructed. "First door on the left." Then he retreated back into his gathering, giving me free roam of his house. Yet this time, rather than investigating the nooks and crawl spaces, I headed directly into Priscilla's room. She was seated at her desk, again examining a street map; my appearance didn't appear either to surprise or to disturb her.

"Papa's planning quite a show for the Aldermen tonight. We should start scalping tickets," said Priscilla—and it took me a moment to register that she was joking. "He's invited McFlythe's great-granddaughter to speak. I'm just kicking myself that I'll have to miss all the fireworks."

"My father's making us go. As a family," I said. "I'll give you a full report."

"You can't go. We already have plans."

Priscilla clearly didn't understand my father. "I don't have a choice."

"Of course, you have a choice. You may have to accept the consequences, but you do have a choice," she replied. "And I need your help tonight. Everyone on this street is going to be at that meeting. It's the best opportunity we'll ever have."

"You can't be serious. Didn't you see the paper? They're doubling police patrols of the area."

I wanted to add: *and innocent motorists nearly got killed last night.* Yet I sensed that line of attack wouldn't further my cause.

"That's why tonight's our night," she said. "It's the one night we can be positive the police won't be out, because they'll need them at City Hall for the meeting. We can go big this time, Josh. Stop signs. Traffic lights. Even the Hutchinson High scoreboard."

"Please," I begged. "I can't. Not tonight."

"Tell them you're sick again. Pretend you twisted your ankle," she ordered. "Come on, Josh. Don't let me down."

"It's not a good idea. Someone is going to get hurt."

"Fine. Whatever." Priscilla swiveled around on her chair. "If you're not going to help me, I'll have to recruit somebody else."

"Maybe next week," I offered. "After things settle down."

"I don't want to hear it. Get out of here," commanded Priscilla. "I'm going to plan on meeting you in the shelter at eight o'clock tonight. If you don't show up, it's your choice—but I'll consider that the end of our partnership."

She folded her arms across her chest and spun her chair toward the wall.

⸺⫷◆⫸⸺

Up until the very moment when the dining room clock struck eight, I genuinely entertained the notion of sneaking down the back steps and meeting Priscilla. In the end, with my father's warning about "oil mixing best with oil" still fresh in my ears, I didn't have the nerve to disappoint him.

My old man had spent most of the afternoon in front of the bathroom mirror, practicing his speech. I still remember the ending: *We're not here to make a political point. We're not here to make an ideological statement. We're here because we live on this street and we deserve a say in what we call it.* On my mother's advice, he also added some levity, including the line, *If accuracy is so essential, I'd be more than delighted to put up the money to purchase a hutch of rabbits.* He left the house after supper to confer with several like-minded colleagues. "I like the bow tie," my mother reassured him as he departed, pecking him on the lips. "Give 'em hell, Harry."

We drove downtown two hours later, south on Rabbit Meadow Lane, past the darkened windows of the Pozner residence, then left onto Van Buren and into the business district. I wore the three-piece cotton suit that my mother had purchased me for Easter services. The collar chafed my neck. In my lap, I cradled my baby sister—this was in the era before mandatory car seats—letting her squeeze her tiny fists around my index fingers. "If that friend of yours is present tonight," warned my mother, "I'd prefer you kept your distance. You should be civil, of course. But there's no need to upset your father unnecessarily." I nearly announced Priscilla wouldn't be there, catching myself at the last moment. When we did arrive at City Hall—a rococo, Gilded Age structure that dominated Woolsey Plaza—it felt as though Priscilla was the only resident of Creve Coeur not in attendance. A standing-room-only crowd occupied the gallery, but my father had reserved us seats behind the press table.

I'd been to a few board meetings as a child, but those had been run-of-the-mill administrative sessions played out before a handful of civic-minded codgers. That night, Bernard Pozner and Tarwell Shuttlesworth had filled the meeting hall: every nonwhite inhabitant of the city must have been present, as well as scores of university students and even a group of Carmelite nuns from a convent in New Bedford. Pozner's activists occupied the northern section of the gallery, opposite the aisle from our own neighbors—like feuding in-laws separated at a wedding. Dr. Weldon's was the only black face on our side. To an outsider, the imagery would have appeared unmistakable.

Chet Chapin called the meeting to order at precisely nine o'clock. The tax attorney represented the most posh sections of Creve Coeur, including the estates across the harbor on Whitmore Boulevard. He spoke with an accent as patrician as Franklin Roosevelt's, dropping his final r's, and rhyming "rather" with "father." The chairman spoke briefly on the intricate processes through which the need for an emergency session arose, referring to several obscure statutes and to Bernard Pozner's petition. Then he yielded the floor to Priscilla's father, as the pair had apparently prearranged, and Pozner passed the microphone to Elizabeth Albion McFlythe. My father objected. The actual phrase he used was, "Leo Lippitt isn't going to let anyone—not even Chet Chapin—sell him down the river." His former ally ignored him. McFlythe's great-granddaughter, a svelte, copper-skinned woman of about fifty, launched into an impassioned plea on behalf of inclusion and unity. She praised her forebear as "our common heritage," sounding as sensible as a bank president. From that moment forward, everyone but my father realized that he didn't stand a chance.

McFlythe concluded with a quotation from Norman Vincent Peale. When the cheers died down, Chet Chapin recognized my father, who drew tepid applause from the partisans of Rabbit Meadow.

My old man adjusted his spectacles. He tested the microphone. He asked for assurances that his audience could hear him. And then he delivered an address that, following on the heels of his opponent's call for interracial dialogue and solidarity, made him sound pretty and insular. The breaking point occurred when he declared, *If accuracy is so essential, I'd be more than delighted to put up the money to purchase a hutch of rabbits.* Nobody laughed. Instead, a college student shouted: *You wouldn't welcome black people like those rabbits!* And another spectator cried out: *Go buy yourself some black folks!*

Chet Chapin called for order. My father broke off his speech.

"Leo Lippitt won't tolerate being insulted," he said firmly. "You should be ashamed of yourselves. All of you." He glared at Chet Chapin and asked, "Have you no sense of decency?" And the audience watched in shock, nobody making a sound as he removed his hat from the coat rack, buttoned his raincoat methodically, and strode up the center aisle toward the door. I looked to my mother, uncertain whether we should follow, but she held me back. My father would want a firsthand report of what ensued.

After that, several of our neighbors spoke—one suggesting that the street could embrace both names, another requesting a six-month delay to accommodate his home-based export business. Several aldermen discussed their concerns about politicizing routine administrative matters, such as the naming of streets, warning the public that whatever decision was reached would not set a precedent.

It was nearly midnight when the Creve Coeur Board of Aldermen voted 7–1, with three abstentions and one absence, to rename the thoroughfare known as Rabbit Meadow Lane after poet Algernon McFlythe.

-◄◄◄◆►►►-

To this day, I don't know whether Priscilla Pozner found someone to help her that night or whether she acted alone—and since she ended her own life several years ago, after what her obituary in the *Sentinel* called "a long struggle," I will likely never learn. I'm not sure it matters. What I do know with certainty is that among the sixteen stop signs she decapitated in less than two hours that night were four located at the intersection of Rabbit Way and Maple that would have kept a Tierney Falls grandmother from plowing her Lincoln into the driver's side of my father's Buick. We rode past the crash site on the way home, oblivious to our loss. Although my father wasn't technically dead then—not yet. He survived another forty-one days in a coma before the neurologists at Methodist Hospital allowed my mother to detach his ventilator.

No more signs disappeared in Creve Coeur after that. I didn't return to school during those forty-one days, and I didn't reveal Priscilla's secret, because it was also my own secret, but I woke each morning through that long summer hoping she might appear at our door to plead for forgiveness. Sometimes, I fantasized she'd deposit the pilfered signs on our steps as an offering, or even that she'd covertly replace the new "Algernon McFlythe Street" tags with their Rabbit Meadow predecessors, in an attempt to make amends for the horrific events she'd set in motion. She never did.

When I shipped out to boarding school in New Hampshire the next autumn, at my own insistence—Chatsworth Hall had been my father's alma mater—I sensed that I'd never see Priscilla again. I'd pursue a career in archaeology, settling on the West Coast, and she'd vanish into the shadows of a world that no longer existed, if it ever had. She'd fade from the neighbor who'd killed my father, to a girl I'd kissed once, to a person I'd known in my youth, a stranger who lived on a street with a meaningless name.

A Change of Plumage

-‹‹‹◆›››-

He had accepted an invitation to lecture on the classification of songbirds, a subject about which he knew absolutely nothing. The address was being jointly sponsored by the Nebraska Chapter of the National Audubon Society and the Ornithological Institute of Omaha; they were willing to pay $5,000 plus expenses. He could picture these heartland bush-thwackers on the edges of their seats, all binoculars and tweed, raising the roof beams for celebrated field guide author and all-around avian expert Bill Grubb. What they'd actually get was perennially cash-strapped Jack Artwell, adjunct creative writing instructor at Gulf Coast Community College and part-time tele-marketer of Cross pens and silver-plated kaleidoscopes, but they'd never know the difference. He'd shake a few hands, say this one's an ostrich, that one's an eagle, and pocket the money.

Bill Grubb had suggested the idea himself. The ornithologist had suffered a debilitating attack of heartbreak and Jack had gone next door to console him—also to deliver the letter and complain about the loud music. Their confrontation took place on Grubb's patio. Thistle and cig-arette butts canopied the flagstone. More butts were piled in the earthenware pot of a desiccated geranium and tucked into the hand-painted hollow gourds that served as bird feeders. Through the open glass doors Edith Piaf crooned "Non, Je Ne Regrette Rien" at top volume, as she had done every morning for nearly a month, frightening away the wildlife and frustrating the neighbors, while the ornithologist paced in endless circles like a mechanical toy gone berserk. Grubb had welcomed Jack with a frown of contagious agony.

"Come to join in on the misery, have you, Artwell?" he demanded. "Well, there's certainly enough of it to go around. Pull up a chair. Wallow. Mope. See firsthand how the high and mighty have fallen."

Jack did not sit down. The loves of Grubb's life, the women of his childhood dreams, had deserted him one too many times: spa attendants picked up at bowling alleys, usherettes lured away from the Cormorant Island Shakespeare Festival. Who had the patience for such mush and histrionics? Those were luxuries that only tenure and sabbatical could buy. The truth of the matter was that he'd befriended Grubb before he really knew him, two junior faculty members exiled to the bogs of the Southwest Florida, that for fifteen years he'd spectated from a shaky perch while Grubb soared above the groves of academe and feathered his nest with television appearances and mass-market publications. Although Jack felt obliged to comfort his grieving neighbor, he refused to mean what he said. He remained standing because he associated sitting down with sincerity.

"I have good news and bad news," said Jack. "Which do you want first?"

"I want Loretta back," answered Grubb.

"That's beyond my control," Jack said, politically. "The bad news is that our nitwit letter carrier left your mail in our box again. But the good news is that you've been invited to some conference in Nebraska for $5,000. I know it's not Loretta—but it's a hell of a lot of money."

Grubb snapped the invitation from Jack's hand. He scanned it quickly, squeezed the letter and envelope in opposite fists as though exercising his fingers, then threw both paper balls over his shoulders into the shrubbery. "Fucking songbirds," he shouted, kicking over a sack of millet. "Who the hell cares about songbirds? I want to talk about birds of prey, vultures like the cock-sucker who stole Loretta. Do you hear me, Artwell? Vultures! You've never had your heart torn out, have you, Artwell?"

Jack retrieved the crumpled letter. He wanted to contradict Grubb, to serve up harrowing tales of lovesickness, but he'd been married for twenty-two years. Half his life. Although he'd broken up with a college girlfriend—she eventually married an oncologist—Gloria had long since nagged away any lingering memories of heartbreak.

"That's good news?" Grubb continued. "What am I supposed to do with $5,000, Artwell? Buy a new Loretta? If it's worth so much to you, you go deliver their goddamned lecture. Why the hell not? You're already reading my mail. You might as well be me. You're probably boffing Loretta on the side, anyway, so why not be able to afford her?"

Jack had endured this stormy cycle before: the thunderclaps of rage and gushing apologies that would produce a floral arrangement for the Artwells' dining room. As though Grubb could purchase his forgiveness with a basket of gladiolus. Gloria always joked that the next time he should demand compensation that wouldn't wilt. Cold, hard cash. Her suggestions would have been more amusing if they hadn't been living paycheck to paycheck on her grade-school librarian's salary, if he didn't waste his afternoons hawking monogrammed inkwells and chalcedony geodes to credulous senior citizens. After fifteen years of feigned friendship, didn't he deserve more? Why not take his due? As Grubb condemned him for all of the things he'd done with Loretta—some of which he had never tried with Gloria, some of which he couldn't even visualize—Jack folded the invitation into his breast pocket.

"It will be fun," he told Gloria at dinner. "Like the plot of a suspense movie."

She pushed her plate to the center of the table. "What am I supposed to do when they lock you up and throw away the key? I truly don't understand what you have against going into business with my brother."

Her brother—his lackluster brother-in-law—distributed commercial adhesives.

"There's nothing illegal about it," he said, patting her hand. "And I won't get caught."

Then he'd gone upstairs to the attic to search through his father's effects for a copy of the *Peterson Field Guide to Birds of North America*.

That first week he studied finches: sparrows, crossbills, grosbeaks. He printed the names of the species on index cards, English on one side, Latin on the other, as though studying a foreign language. It didn't do him any good; all the sparrows looked identical. In frustration he moved on to simpler families, to races with few species and distinctive markings, feeding his confidence on the striking scarlet plumage of the tanagers and the stately epaulets of the waxwings—but there were more than thirty varieties of tanagers, common and cedar and Bohemian waxwings! His determination grew obsessive: magpies clawed at his sanity; warblers trilled him to insomnia; thrushes and robins and wrens fluttered between his ears. He walked down to the municipal park each afternoon to study and feed breadcrumbs to the pigeons—he still knew a pigeon when he saw one—but after six hours of cramming he'd discover that he'd fallen for some taxonomical misnomer, that morning warblers weren't actually warblers at all. Or he'd come across magpie-robins! Or wren-thrushes! Memorizing fingerprints would have been easier.

As if nature hadn't made his task arduous enough, everyone he knew seemed hell-bent on making it more difficult. Distractions swarmed around him like cattle birds. First there was Gloria, always breathing down his neck, badgering him about finances. She'd quote the exact balance in their checking account three times during the course of one meal. Or he'd retreat into their backyard at dusk to apply his knowledge, and she'd stare at him through the bay windows like the Ghost of Christmas Past. His neighbor's antics were equally frustrating. Grubb's death throes continued until Jack began to experience surges of vicarious depression. Not only did he have to overdose daily on Edith Piaf and profanity, but he also had to conduct his forays into the backyard in full view of the ornithologist. That meant no binoculars, no birdcalls. Nothing that might raise suspicion. He contemplated purchasing a croquet set as a decoy. Instead he sent his wife next door to distract the old coot. What better way—and he congratulated himself on the phrasing—to kill two birds with one stone.

His other principal distraction was Introduction to Poetry and Prose. Three sections at $1,500 each. Four mornings a week he drove out to Gulf Coast Community and taught the mute inglorious Miltons of the next generation the difference between simile and metaphor. His students swallowed knowledge like funnels; they were petrified stumps lacquered with rouge and mascara. After years of assigning the same exercises—describe an orange, describe an orange from the point of view of a citrus farmer, from the point of view of a Cuisinart—he considered upping the ante. Why not have them describe a corporate office from the point of view of the coffee maker? Or compose a happy ending to *Anna Karenina*? Or rewrite *Moby-Dick* without references to whales? The money—that's why not. Irreverence costs just as much as heartbreak. If he got himself fired, Gloria would go through the rafters. While someday he might tell his human funnels to rework *The Sound and The Fury* in the style of James Joyce, making appropriate allusions to Dublin, for now he drooled over their citrus epics. Only once—how could he resist—he asked them to describe a symposium on songbirds from the point of view of a writer. Their lack of specialized knowledge astounded him.

The next morning—week three—he shared their ignorance with Gloria. His wife was wearing her threadbare purple bathrobe, struggling with the crossword puzzle. She gnawed on a pencil stub while she thought; small bits of eraser were wedged between her teeth. For a split second—when he complained that his students didn't know a titmouse from a dormouse—he perceived her from the vantage point of a stranger: as a bone-weary middle-aged librarian.

"Why are you doing this, Jack?" she asked.

"Because I want to," he answered. "To prove I can."

"What do you hope to accomplish? Is it about the money?"

"It's about birds," he said. "Birds *and* money."

It wasn't, of course, about birds *or* money. Not really. He did have his moments of pleasure, such as when, after years of teaching Keats, he discovered what nightingales and skylarks actually looked like, but for the most part he found songbirds brain-numbingly boring. Good for shitting on park benches and stuffing into pillows, but not much else. What appealed to him was stepping out of his own skin for a little while, molting into somebody else. But how to explain that to Gloria? How to explain that what he really wanted was a dose of adventure, a chance to hoodwink a pack of strangers and maybe make an ass out of Bill Grubb in the process? She wanted money, children. He wanted a story to tell his grandkids. And—to tell the truth—he didn't mind the money. Five grand wasn't *that* much—but if he could pull it off once, he could do it again and again. Why the hell not?

So he made travel arrangements, cataloged grackles. He'd allotted himself a daily quota of species in the Peterson guide, but as B-Day approached, he abandoned it. Instead he drove out to Gulf Coast City to explore the exotic birdhouse at the zoo, then rented Hitchcock's *The Birds* and held the tape on pause while he tested his knowledge. Gradually he rationalized himself into a position of expertise. It isn't what I know, he thought. It's what they know. And how much could a flock of Midwestern retirees and their wives possibly know about taxonomy? He'd be dealing with the sort of folks who got duped on *Candid Camera*. Easy as pie.

He didn't even bother to write out his speech.

It would be more challenging, he laughed, to wing it.

He changed planes in Kansas City, took a commuter flight into Omaha. It was a fourteen-seat Cessna, just small enough for midair solidarity to develop, so he presented himself as Bill Grubb to a motley sampling of commodities lawyers and retired soybean farmers. Among the passengers was a pharmaceuticals executive and zealous bird-watcher who carried a copy of *Grubb's Songbirds* in his attaché case. Rubber bands secured the dog-eared pages. *Only two books worth having,* said the executive. *Grubb's and the New Testament. They come with me everywhere. I'm always telling Mrs. Coolidge that an autographed copy of either one would make my lifetime.* The executive laughed raucously; Jack resisted the urge to sign both. He scrawled Grubb's name with a flourish. Only later did he suffer the twinge of panic, instantly followed by a surge of relief, when he realized that his neighbor's photograph didn't appear anywhere on the jacket cover. Then he thought of Grubb's television appearances, on public broadcasting, on the Discovery Channel. But who could remember a talking head? All they'd remember was a forty-something chain-smoker in a dark suit. He found a newsstand at Eppley Field and purchased a pack of Winstons, smoked his first cigarette in ten years, enjoyed the sensation of his head rising like a circus tent. Being somebody else had its privileges.

The conference director, Dr. Burbank, had suggested they meet outside the baggage claim, near the shoeshine stand. Jack scanned the sea of harried business travelers and vacationing families, waiting for his ride, but none of the middle-aged men in the crowd appeared to be looking for a passenger. The only person near the shoeshine stand was a striking and decidedly un-ornithological young woman. She stood uncomfortably among the cabbies and chauffeurs, holding a cardboard sign reading Grubb, as though panhandling for food. Long ginger hair cascaded over her shoulders and the top two buttons of her cotton blouse were undone. Dark glasses shielded her eyes. Jack searched the crowd for Dr. Burbank, the director of the institute, but his gaze kept returning magnetically to the young woman. The mistake hit him with the force of a boiler explosion: he *was* Grubb. The girl was waiting for him. There would be no doddering bird expert with a sign reading Artwell.

He stepped directly in front of the woman and they stared at each other.

"Dr. Grubb?" she finally asked.

"The one and only."

"Grace Burbank."

He stiffened. Was it possible that they were on to him, that they'd dispatched their own imposter as part of some midwestern joke? He'd spoken to Burbank on the telephone. Twice. The ornithologist had rasped in a voice that was possibly emphysemic, but unquestionably male. Jack grazed the woman's extended fingers and waited to be exposed; a lit cigarette somehow found its way to his mouth.

"You're not Dr. Burbank," he ventured.

The woman smiled and steered them through the crowd.

"Did you really think they'd send the director of the institute to meet a criminal?"

"What do you mean?" he snapped.

"I mean you're not above the law."

"And you're not Dr. Burbank," he retorted, fighting fire with fire. "So we're even."

The woman responded with a high-pitched ripple. "There's nothing illegal about impersonating an ornithologist, you know."

Jack sensed the charge in his abdomen, in his bladder. His accuser stepped through the revolving doors of the terminal and crossed the traffic plaza into the parking garage. His legs followed her obediently, sweat fusing his trousers to the insides of his thighs. He anticipated battalions of armed park rangers on horseback, maybe the Royal Canadian Mounted Police. Or would they call in the FBI for an interstate felon? In either case, his goose was cooked. He needed to make a break for it. Now or never. His eyes fled behind dumpsters, over concrete parapets, but his body kept walking. It was one thing to flee snipers and swat teams, quite another to desert a redheaded bombshell. He'd been outsmarted.

The girl stopped suddenly in front of a blue Honda Civic. An old-fashioned paddy wagon would have eased Jack's nerves. He wanted the torture to end.

"So what happens now?" he asked, trying to sound nonchalant. "If I confess outright, do I avoid the rack and the thumbscrews?"

"Confessions won't do you any good," retorted the girl. "But don't worry. We'll spare you the thumbscrews. The last guy only got twenty years."

"*Twenty-years?*"

"It'll make you think twice before you light up in an airport again," said the girl. "I don't know how you do things in Florida, but this is Nebraska. Government buildings are off limits—stores and hotel lobbies, too. *And my car.*"

Jack steadied himself against the vehicle, the blood returning to his stomach. So that was all. Since he'd quit smoking, the rules of the game had changed. How stupid to imagine she was onto him—to risk giving himself away! He had to be more careful.

"But you're not Dr. Burbank," he said.

"My father's overwhelmed with the conference and all. Last-minute stuff. You know how birders are, all fuss and feathers, so you'll have to make do with me. But I promise I won't bite. Since you can't check into your room yet, I thought you'd like to cruise over to the National Grasslands for a peek at the meadowlarks. What do you say, Dr. Grubb?"

"Burbank's daughter," Jack repeated, breathless. "I didn't expect—"

"And who *did* you expect?" fired Grace Burbank. "Dorothy Gale?"

⋘◆⋙

The girl kept Jack on the defensive for the remainder of the afternoon. She was working toward a doctorate in vertebrate zoology at the state university, writing a dissertation on the mating habits of quail—a topic upon which Grubb had apparently penned the definitive treatise. Unfortunately, quail weren't songbirds, but fowl, so Jack knew nothing about them. He'd never even been bird-watching before—not unless one counted the excursions into his own backyard—and Burbank's daughter was grilling him on the intricacies of partridge foreplay. She wanted his expertise, also his approval. As though his opinions regarding the courtship rituals of sand grouse had any effect on what actually happened in the prairie grass. How the hell was he supposed to know why male ptarmigans formed alliances with other male ptarmigans when searching for mates? Maybe the birds were insecure, he thought. Or bisexual. If Burbank's daughter had been any less attractive, he'd have told her to compose a happy ending for *Anna Karenina*.

"You're so quiet, Dr. Grubb," Grace finally said. "So modest. You think my theory about the ptarmigans is way off base, don't you? Shoot me down. I can take it."

"I've become a liberal in my old age," Jack answered. "What ptarmigans do in their own nests is none of my business. If they're consenting adults, that is."

Grace's flashed him a ribbon of delicate white teeth.

"Seriously," she said. "Do you think my argument holds water?"

The girl flipped up her shades; her eyes waltzed nervously. Jack looked away. They stood alone on a blanket of prairie grass, hemmed between crested buttes. Redwing blackbirds glided toward the horizon. The foliage echoed in their ears. If only I really were Grubb, thought Jack, then I'd have her answers. That wasn't what he meant. He knew that if he really were Grubb, if Gloria wasn't waiting for him back in Florida, he wouldn't need the answers. Then fear cut short his reverie. Somehow the conference organizers knew Grubb wasn't married or they would have sent an invitation for two. Jack clasped his hands behind his back. "Isn't that a meadowlark?" he asked, too forcefully. When the girl turned away, he slipped his wedding ring into his pocket.

"I don't see anything," said Grace. "Say, you haven't been listening to a word I've said, have you? You're not taking me seriously! You think I'm just some amateur from out in the sticks full of hair-brained speculations. But I guess that's my fault. Why would *you* be interested in my silly hypothesis?" The anger sparked across her face. Then the girl was trembling, bleeding tears.

"Your ideas are brilliant," said Jack.

She continued to sob.

"I'm so sorry, Dr. Grubb. It's just that I've been working so hard."

"Truly brilliant," he repeated—and he believed his own words.

"You don't mean that," answered Grace.

He could hear the hope in her voice.

"Honestly, Grace," he said. "Your theories are as good as anything I've ever come up with. Probably better—but let's keep that between us."

He offered her his handkerchief; she wiped her eyes. If her vulnerability hadn't faded so quickly, he might have taken her in his arms. Seconds later—when she turned the tables—he longed for the lost opportunity. No sooner had the girl blown her nose than she was pitching another theory, as sassy as ever, this one regarding the classification of the passenger pigeon. Only passenger pigeons were extinct—and the Peterson guide didn't include historic species. Jack sensed his own nerves unwinding, his need for the handkerchief mounting. Burbank's daughter was beyond sexy. She was relentless.

"Let's walk a little farther," he said. "We'll talk more later."

So they walked. They strolled the wooden boardwalks until their shadows played into the distant crimson buttes, always side by side, never touching. An occasional birdwatcher crossed their path: two elderly women wearing matching sun visors, a long-haired young man with a wooden staff. Otherwise they were alone with the jackrabbits and cotton moths. Jack steered their conversation away from ornithology and they discussed Willa Cather novels and the awe experienced by the first pioneers. Then they spoke about the solitude of the prairie—about the edge of the earth. It wasn't until that evening, when Jack returned to the hotel and signed his neighbor's name in the register, that he realized he had forgotten about his upcoming lecture. Other fears had taken over.

Jack no longer questioned his feelings for the girl. He was Bill Grubb, at least in Nebraska, at least for the weekend—and Bill Grubb was single. This only increased his anxiety because he knew that his own consent was the easier half of the battle.

He stretched out, fully clothed, on the sanitized bed.

"After the conference," he said aloud. "Who'll ever know?"

He wrapped his wedding ring in his handkerchief and deposited the white cloth on the end table. Carrying the ring, even in his pocket, made him nervous. It never paid to be too careful. Then he stared at the rag for several seconds, puzzled, before retrieving the ring and stuffing the empty handkerchief—monogram and all—under his mattress.

-◄◄◄◆►►►-

Three hundred bush-thwackers turned out for his lecture. They sat on folding chairs in the gymnasium of Wendell Wilkie High School. Posters of California condors and whooping cranes did their best to conceal the wall mats, and a mammoth papier-mâché eagle hung from a pair of stationary rings overhead. Dr. Burbank explained that the state numismatists convention had commandeered all of the local convention space. *Money talks*, chimed the reedy ornithologist. Then he leaned into the speaker's ear and added, *Try to make it short. There's a volleyball tournament scheduled for three o'clock.* Jack tried to look glum.

He stepped up to the podium—which bore a striking resemblance to a vaulting horse—and cleared his throat. The audience applauded politely. Mostly older couples, but not nearly as gaunt as he'd expected. Overalls. Flannel Shirts. No tweed. A few of the spectators carried notepads; others used their programs as fans. This could have been the annual meeting of the Chamber of Commerce or the County Grange. Jack cleared his throat again. He'd planned to draft a lecture the previous evening. Instead he'd spent the night fantasizing about Burbank's daughter, wondering what she'd be like in bed, wondering whether he would find out, hoping she'd let him try some of the things Grubb accused him of doing to Loretta. Now he dreaded calling out her name on impulse.

"Songbirds," he said. "Songbirds."

His audience leaned forward. He had nothing to say.

"I know you were all expecting a lecture on the classification of song-birds, but you're not going to get one. What kind of man would I be if I shook a couple of hands, said this one's an ostrich, that one's an eagle, and pocketed your money? I respect you too much for that."

The bush-thwackers drew a collective breath. They stopped fanning their programs.

"I'm not the expert you think I am," he continued. "I don't know the first thing about birds. The truth of the matter is that I'm an imposter. All I'd be good for is a handful of indecent jokes about bisexual ptarmigans."

Color drained from some faces, bloated others. An audience of snow geese and cardinals. Owen Burbank, holding his hands to his temples, became a giant scarlet tanager. The stillness was taxidermic.

"Who did I think I was fooling?" asked Jack. "When Grace Burbank, Dr. Burbank's daughter, picked me up at Eppley Field yesterday, I realized that I'd never be able to deceive you. Certainly not with one of the leading ornithological minds in the world sitting in the audience. That's why I'd like to invite Grace Burbank to join me for a dialogue on the mating habits of prairie fowl. Her work on quail makes even yours truly, Bill Grubb, feel like an ignorant imposter."

The bush-thwackers exhaled into glee. Grace shielded her mouth with her hand, shook her head vigorously, and then staggered toward the vaulting horse. Her eyes exuded gratitude.

"Sorry about that, friends," he said to the audience. "I didn't mean to frighten you."

The papier-mâché eagle swayed to laughter and applause.

—⫷◆⫸—

That night she showed up at his hotel room like a homing pigeon. All he'd had to do was give Grace the room number after their lecture, suggest that she might want to drop by to wish him farewell. No innuendo, no advances. Jack was so certain she'd come to him that he phoned the airline and postponed his departing flight. *It's a special opportunity*, he told Gloria. *They want me to do a study on mating habits.* One final call, to room service, produced a bottle of chilled champagne. This is what they mean by a bird in hand, thought Jack. Time to show her who's Dorothy Gale and who's the cyclone. The girl had hardly thanked him for all that he'd done— particularly his willingness to let her dominate their dialogue—before he had her skirt bunched around her hips.

"Were you frightened?" he asked, afterwards, smoking a Winston.

She ran the back of her hand across his chest. "Frightened?"

"When I told the audience I was an imposter."

"Not for a minute," she said.

"You should have seen your father. He looked as though his arteries were about to tear down the seams. I wonder what he would have done if I really had been an imposter."

"There would have been hell to pay," said Grace. "A couple of years ago he got into a dispute at a conference and tried to strangle a botanist. Ornithologists can be pretty damn temperamental."

"And you?" Jack asked.

"Me?"

"What would you have done if I wasn't me? If I were just some ordinary sap."

"You could never be ordinary," answered the girl. "Besides, I guess I planned on falling for you even before I met you. I feel like I've been in love with you for years—that every night I spent in the college library reading your primer on migration was part of our courtship. How couldn't I recognize you?"

They nuzzled on the bed for another hour and then Jack drifted into sleep. In his dreams he was no longer impersonating an ornithologist, but an emperor. Thousands of sexy young women succumbed to his spell and he had to fight them off with his scepter. Jack didn't know how long this dream lasted—seconds or hours. It ended abruptly in pain.

"You're an imposter!" she shouted. "A fraud!"

Her fists pounded into his back and shoulders. Jack rolled onto his stomach, deflecting the blows as best he could, and switched on the lamp. The light at the far end of the room was already on and a book lay folded across the seat of a chair. Grace was fully clothed.

"I thought you said it wouldn't matter," said Jack.

She hit him harder, drove her talons into his throat.

"How could it not matter?" cried Grace. "You bastard! I loved you!"

"Calm down," pleaded Jack. "It's okay."

"It's not okay. Let me see your hands."

The girl pried open his fists. He feared she was going to bend back his fingers, but the girl simply stared at them for several seconds and then tensed as though shot. He tried to catch her on the way out the door, but gave up at the threshold. He couldn't run through the corridors naked. Half-sleep misted his thoughts. How did an ornithologist's hands differ from a writer's hands? he wondered. And what was he to do now?

Jack turned back to the empty room and realized that he didn't have to do anything. His secret—his *big* secret—remained safe. The sights that had frightened away Burbank's daughter were the most reassuring Jack had ever seen: a band of white skin circling one of his fingers and his wedding ring glistening like a parrot's eye on the nightstand.

⸻◦⸻

The next morning Jack rode a taxi out to the airstrip. The driver, grizzled under an engineer's cap, colored their surroundings in a voice as flat as the prairie. *I know my Omaha*, he bragged. *Lead smelting, hog feed, insurance. You learn a lot taking folks from place to place. And what you don't learn*, he added, his face florid with conspiracy, *you can always make up.* The driver's last observation flowed into a chuckling fit. *Isn't that the way*, answered Jack. *There's one born every minute.* Then he introduced himself as Dr. Owen Burbank of the Ornithological Institute. Why the hell not? He was ripe for a change of plumage.

Jack rolled down the cab window, savored the sharp breeze. Nebraska air smelled fresher than Florida air—or maybe it *tasted* fresher—air taps a sense all its own. His lungs swallowed the wheat fields. So these, he thought, were the amber waves of grain. Then his mind drifted across his recent victories, his flawless presentation, the $5,000 check in his breast pocket. And he thought about how he'd one-upped both his wife and his neighbor, his conscience as pure as a nun's wimple, as the coat of an egret. Who'd been hurt? Certainly not Gloria; their checking account balance had tripled. And Grubb couldn't complain. If anything, he'd done the old coot a favor, earned him a reputation for wit among the hayseeds. That left only the girl. At first, Jack wondered whether he hadn't done wrong by Grace, albeit unwittingly, but the alternative would have been worse: How cruel to leave her pining away for a lover who never existed! Besides, *she'd* stormed out on *him*! Didn't he have every right to be heartbroken? What he actually felt was relief—the security of knowing that she no longer had a motive to trace him. He'd leave the melancholy to the Grubbs of the world. Jack Artwell preferred adventure. When he stretched his limbs on the open-air plaza outside the terminal, indulging on one final Winston, he felt his own kicker pounding away like a giant woodpecker in his chest.

The time had arrived for his swan song. As Owen Burbank, Jack convinced the grizzled driver to go back to the Ornithological Institute for payment. *Feel free to run the meter on the return trip,* he offered. The concession made him feel generous. As Bill Grubb, he complained that he knew nothing about a changed reservation and bullied himself onto the next flight. *Are you sure that I telephoned?* he demanded of the desk attendant. *Because I'm sure I didn't phone. Probably an imposter, a practical joke.* As Chuck Coolidge, pharmaceuticals executive, he got several stock tips from a Topeka-based financial planner and a free glass of cognac off a hyenic foundation administrator well beyond her beauty. There was a tight scrape with a hawk-nosed Creighton College alumnus who'd gone to school with a different Chuck Coolidge, a senior vice president at Pfizer, but they ended up bonding over the coincidence. *I've run across him before,* said Jack. *Birdwatcher, religious fellow.* The hawk-nosed man said, *Bible-thumping windbag,* and they swapped stories into Kansas City.

Stepping onto the tarmac in Tallahassee, refreshed, rejuvenated, Jack had only one regret: no one would ever know the extent of his subterfuge. Gloria would be the breadth and depth of his audience—and he'd have to edit out the bit about the girl. This struck him as a cruel injustice, walking away with only five grand and the genus of the arboreal flycatcher ingrained in his soul. What was the point of adventure if one couldn't share it? Holding his malarial secret through Grubb's heartbreak and music would be smoldering torture. The frustration singed his arteries during baggage claim, along the interstate. He hadn't actually one-upped anybody; he had no choice but to live as a bird of paradise, unappreciated, in the land of the blind. Or did he? Jack suddenly realized that there was one person he could tell. Grubb. He'd turn the tables on the old coot, show him that anybody could fill his shoes. And the ornithologist wouldn't dare breathe a word.

"Grubb!" Jack shouted. "Grubb!"

He charged across the wet grass into his neighbor's backyard. That's when he saw them: Sitting beyond the bay windows in his own living room, profiles in the candlelight, embracing to the mournful strains of Edith Piaf. Gloria swayed to the music, her hands wrapped around the ornithologist's bare chest. Jack darted through the flowerbeds. He fumbled with his house keys and dropped them through a ventilation grating. Then he pounded on the windows, hammered fists into the siding, threw his entire weight against the kitchen door. Their music drowned out his desperation. He had no way of getting back inside.

THE DESECRATION
AT LEMMING BAY

-⋘◆⋙-

A second marriage is a matter of cost and benefit. That, at least, was the perspective of seventy-one-year-old Martin Koestler, widower of nineteen months, assiduously reformed Jew, unrepentant Rockefeller Republican, holdout St. Louis Browns fan, amateur paleontologist, former amateur beekeeper, and semiretired owner of the third largest manufacturer of synthetic packaging materials east of the Mississippi. In his case, he had three adult children to consider. Not that his daughters, two architects and a pediatric dentist, didn't stand on their own legs—but both their feelings and their future inheritances weighed in his calculus. So did his baby sister, Sally, clinging to a derelict husband who might evaporate again at any moment. Deep down, after those weeks tending to his wife in her ICU cell, her once-delicate features bloated and tube-riddled, Koestler also dreaded enlisting for an encore round of the emotional travails (to succor, to mourn) that might come with another marriage. Balanced against these interests stood svelte, frisky Joyce Wofford, his beloved Eleanor's oncologist, as well as his impulsive yearning to perform a grand romantic gesture. Koestler did the connubial math one evening in May, on the commuter train from Manhattan to Sedgemoor, and Joyce won out.

After the *whether* had been settled—a process that included a consultation with a highly recommended trusts and estates attorney—Koestler devoted his energies to the *how*. His college roommate, Bud Scheuer, had flown his now third wife to Venice to propose on a gondola, but Koestler suspected that Joyce, who'd been to Italy multiple times with her ex-husband, would be less than impressed by such extravagance. What the occasion demanded, he understood, was a modest yet poignant gesture. He'd asked his youngest daughter—she was the most creative of the lot—for ideas, but she'd suggested a private cruise around Manhattan, which he thought rather cliché. And then, through some perverse mélange of chance and fate, as Koestler walked across his basement one Saturday morning, carrying a replacement lightbulb for the pantry, his eyes fell upon a slender gray volume, *Diphtheria and Other Mementos*, askew on a shelf, and he knew, just *knew*, in that moment, that he would ask for Joyce's hand in the magnolia grove that shaded Isadore Bostwick's tomb.

Koestler often stumbled into life-altering decisions through such flukes. His inspiration for paleontology arose when his late wife's book club read *The French Lieutenant's Woman* and he overheard their dissection of Charles Smithson from the kitchen. He'd taken up beekeeping after a yellow jacket stung his infant granddaughter at a picnic. So when a glimpse of a book that had once meant so much to him—before he'd traded in his literary ambitions for the stability of Styrofoam peanuts—recalled his earlier expedition to the poet's gravesite, Koestler suddenly found himself unable to imagine any other possible venue for proposing than the heights above Lemming Bay. How, he wondered, could he ever have considered anyplace else?

His first visit to Lemming Bay, as a nineteen-year-old sophomore at City College, had occurred on a whim. They'd been reading Bostwick in Professor Roane's Greats of Modern Literature class—Bostwick had been a staple of the canon then, back when there still was a canon—and Bud Scheuer had asked over breakfast, "Anyone want to skip out on Roane the

Drone and see the guy's tomb?" So he'd piled into the back seat of Scheuer's road-weary Buick Invicta, between gaunt Harold Lustgarten and tubby Irv Koppleman, fighting down his nausea while long-legged Dave Barloff, ensconced in the passenger seat, directed the jouncing vehicle toward Rhode Island. Now Scheuer was on his third wife, Koestler reflected, and Dave Barloff was long dead—killed in a turboprop crash outside Tulsa, after joining the Indian Health Service to avoid Vietnam. Harold Lustgarten had done three years in the federal pen for tax evasion and, according to the alumni monthly, operated a bed and breakfast on Sea Island. Koestler had no clue what had become of Irv Koppleman. But he indelibly recalled the five of them standing on the cliffs above Lemming Bay, paying homage to the great poet, as a high school football hero might conjure up glory days on the gridiron to reassure himself that he had lived his life fully—*that he had mattered.*

For a solid ten years between adolescence and his champagne duty in the naval reserve, Bostwick's verse had been Koestler's comrade-in-arms: Bostwick, connoisseur of unmet expectations and mundane disappointments, patron saint of the wistful, the melancholic, the irascibly bittersweet—a lone village crier shouting into the oncoming squall of modernity. The critics who later revived his reputation billed him as the "Jewish Larkin," although to ambivalent and occasionally self-loathing Koestler, that somehow seemed a deprecation, like calling Einstein the "Jewish Bohr." *Diphtheria and Other Mementos* had led Koestler to change his major (briefly) from engineering to English. *Typhoid Is for Lovers* left a welling hollow in his chest.

Joyce Wofford, it turned out, had never heard of Bostwick. "I can probably name three poets, total," she said. And she did. Her triumvirate consisted of Robert Frost, Ogden Nash, and Shel Silverstein. "If you'll count Dr. Seuss and Shakespeare, that's five." Koestler wasn't sure if she was joking, but he didn't dare to ask. "Don't look so alarmed, Mart," she said, gently chucking his chin between her index finger and thumb. "How many chemotherapeutic agents can you name?"

At least a dozen, thought Koestler. *Every poison that you infused into*

Eleanor's veins. But he did not want to ruin the moment, so he kept his tongue in check.

"I would *love* a weekend away," said Joyce. "Rhode Island—or anywhere, for that matter. But Jill will have to agree to look after Mama."

Joyce Wofford's mother lived alone in a fifth floor walkup on West 78th Street. She was ninety-six years old, God bless her. (God bless her until she fractures a hip and dies in agony on her bathroom floor, Koestler occasionally thought, but he did not voice this either.) Koestler's girlfriend—how peculiar to call someone a girlfriend at seventy-one—accompanied the ancient Mrs. Wofford shopping every weekend. The notion of her delegating this responsibility to Jill, his future stepdaughter, a self-styled performance artist with a DWI arrest for each of her three years at community college, struck Koestler as marginally irresponsible. He wouldn't have let the girl within a ten-mile radius of his own mother, rest her unforgiving soul. Yet if his grand romantic gesture cost his future mother-in-law a few days of hunger, so be it. Who ever said love comes cheap?

—«‹•›»—

Between Koestler's professional obligations (the annual meetings of the Association for Packaging & Processing Technologies, the PACK EXPO convention, etc.) and Joyce's on-call schedule at the hospital (at sixty-eight, with an endowed chair, she was the only division chief at St. Dymphna's to cover weekends), the Labor Day holiday proved the first available opportunity for their joint expedition to Lemming Bay. During the wait, Koestler purchased an amethyst and diamond engagement ring with a pavé halo, pleased that he'd thought to learn Joyce's birthstone. Ever practical, he also acquired a third plot alongside his and Eleanor's at Mount Ararat. Joyce, he assured himself, would appreciate such foresight. Koestler's late wife had been an idealistic, vulnerable spirit—shattered by bad news and sheltered with euphemism. His current girlfriend was all earthy pleasures and brass tacks.

The trip itself started without promise. They'd hardly reached New Haven—Koestler at the helm of his Oldsmobile, Joyce flipping through her AAA guide—when she announced, "It's not a grave, Mart. It's a cenotaph."

"What's that?"

"The cenotaph was dedicated in 1957 on the tenth anniversary of the Rhode Island-born poet's death," Joyce read aloud in her rich, crystalline voice. "Bostwick is interred at Beth Abraham Cemetery in Oradell, New Jersey."

The information, as innocent as it might be, slapped Koestler like a personal affront—as though someone had challenged the authenticity of his college diploma or his marriage certificate.

"I could have sworn he was buried there," said Koestler.

"Well, he wasn't," said Joyce. "But truthfully, I'm relieved you didn't know. Otherwise, I'd be spending Labor Day in Oradell, New Jersey."

She smiled at Koestler and he was unable to resist smiling back. Such was Joyce's magic: no matter how appalling the reality, she managed to make life tolerable in its aftermath. Maybe that was why, when she'd hugged him at Eleanor's unveiling, he'd had the audacity to invite her to see his collection of fossils. "Your wife's going to die," she'd warned him nearly two years earlier, "but it's going to be okay." Yet after she'd demoted Bostwick's tomb to a cenotaph, some of the magic of Koestler plan seemed lost to a toxic ether. He flipped the radio to "Swing Down Memory Lane." How strange, he mused, that he now enjoyed the same big band standards that his parents had once danced to in their living room.

"May I?" asked Joyce, reaching for the dial. "Listening to this makes me feel like one of your fossils."

She cut short "There'll Be Bluebirds" mid-bar. A moment later, the vehicle filled with the seductive rhythms of "Pleasant Valley Sunday."

"Hey, that was Kay Kyser," Koestler objected.

"And these are the Monkees," replied Joyce, grinning. "It's time you met them."

"I know those are the Monkees. Davy Jones, right? He's probably the same age as I am."

"Actually, he's dead." She patted his shoulder with a hint of indulgence, possibly condescension. "And that's Micky Dolenz singing. Davy Jones has an English accent."

"You've got me beat. Again," said Koestler.

He tried to sound playful, yet deep down he found himself irritated. He had nothing against the Monkees, or the relentless slew of oldies hits that followed, but it was hard to think straight over the rhythms of the Platters and the Lovin' Spoonful. Joyce must have sensed his mood dip, because she clutched his hand. "It's so good to get away," she said. "Thank you for taking me." He squeezed back gently but said nothing.

They reached New Haven around 10:30, entered Rhode Island shortly after one o'clock and crossed the Jamestown Bridge at 2:15. Along the way, they stopped for coffee at a welcome station and enjoyed a spirit-buoying surprise: at the vending gazebo, two young men in taupe uniforms were unloading cases of soft drinks from a box truck. The foam insets that separated the soda cans from the plastic trays bore the embossment "Koestler Industries." He did not point these out to Joyce, not wishing to appear self-important, yet he hoped she might notice. He recalled a moment, many years earlier, when he'd been driving Amy's carpool—subbing, while Eleanor recovered from her hysterectomy—and he'd trumpeted a Koestler-brand dumpster in the parking lot opposite the girls' ice skating rink. His daughter had practically died of shame.

"I should buy a postcard for Mama," said Joyce. "And a T-shirt for Jill."

She did not mention a word about the Koestler insets.

"And for me? Don't I get a present?"

Joyce ran her nails across his abdomen. "You'll get your present later."

⁻⧓⧓◆⧓⧓⁻

Koestler had booked them a suite at a colonial inn above the Maidstone River. Baskets of squash and calico corn nestled on wrought-iron stands framing the French door; a painstakingly carved serpent, armed with an apple, coiled up the astragal between its leaves. Inside, the lobby smelled of woodchips and peppermint. A military macaw perched silently in a colossal cage behind the registration desk, where a pair of women—one pushing twenty, the other nearly as old as the inn, both rafter-tall with matching bony faces—flashed wary smiles. The girl's expression grew more welcoming when Koestler announced, "We have a reservation." About the only blight on the rustic setting was a young couple chatting on the nearby sofa. The man wore a seersucker suit; his date sported burgundy heels, but also piercings through her septum and chin. Koestler identified the pair as guests at a wedding he was grateful not to be attending.

"Take a look at that fellow," whispered Koestler. "He looks like the kind of guy who gets his shoes shined at the airport."

Joyce swatted his behind with her palm. "Behave yourself," she said.

"And she looks like my daughter's friend who moved to Portland, Oregon," he said. "You have to admire Portland. Middle-aged people all over the country work their asses off so their children can retire to Portland."

"I said behave," replied Joyce, mock stern, "or no dessert for you."

A moment later, the skeletal-featured girl escorted them up to their chamber. She turned down the vast, quilt-lacquered bed and Koestler tipped her five dollars. The afternoon sun formed a glowing white grid on the throw rug.

Koestler stepped to the windows. Out on the Maidstone River, teenagers splashed in a mayhem of canoes and swan dives and dogpaddling. He drew shut both sets of blinds.

"So," he said. "We're here. When do I get my dessert?"

Joyce laughed. "After dinner," she said. Yet she drew toward him and wrapped her arms around his torso.

How ravishing she looked—even after four hours on the interstate. She wasn't beautiful *for sixty-eight*; she was just beautiful. Yet you could also detect the vestiges of the seductive, almost feral visage that had once spawned whistles from workmen and rendered college boys mute. Koestler yearned to drop to one knee on the spot and to brandish the gemstones. He thought of Bostwick's grave—or cenotaph—and immediately recalled the final lines of the poet's *Polio Serenade*: "So be not accused of dither or delay / If you could screw it up tomorrow, you can screw it up today." No need to hurry, he told himself. I made a game plan and I'll follow it. Besides, the ring still lay tucked inside his travel bag, locked in the trunk of the Oldsmobile.

"I love you," he said.

"I love you too," replied Joyce. "And do you know what else I love? I love how we can escape together like this and then go back home and lead our own separate lives."

Koestler felt slashed with a blade. Did she suspect his intentions? Could she really be trying to ward him off? Or was she merely striking a nonpossessive pose, reassuring him that she didn't seek more than he was willing to offer? He'd started dating Eleanor at sixteen; they'd been too smitten for any psychological grappling. Forced to confront the female psyche for the first time in his seventh decade, Koestler felt like a Neanderthal discovering fire.

"Does that mean you'd be indifferent to a marriage proposal from a wealthy widower?" he ventured.

He strove to sound as though he were joking, but that led Joyce to respond in kind.

"I much prefer my men impoverished and married. I'm holding out for a life of squalor and bigamy." She clutched his sweater and tugged him close, her full lips only inches from his. "Now what was that you said about passing up dinner and skipping straight to dessert?"

-‹‹‹•›››-

The weather the following morning boded poorly: a raw, lancing breeze chilled the air with mist off the bay. Herring gulls circled malevolently overhead. Damp leaves clung to the windshield of the Oldsmobile, gumming up the wipers. Koestler had insisted they take their continental breakfast to go—determined to beat any other tourists to the alleged cenotaph. It was only eight o'clock, still plenty of time for the haze to burn off. What he wanted was a crisp, autumn day like the one that he'd enjoyed from Bud Scheuer's Buick. His nerves buzzed as he contemplated what lay ahead.

"I hope we beat the crowds," needled Joyce, nibbling her croissant. "Maybe you should drop me off so I can reserve us a place in line."

"Can't you please humor me for once?" he asked—not in a banterous mood. "It's truly one of the most sublime places on earth."

"I *am* humoring you," she replied. "If I wasn't humoring you, I'd still be asleep."

She reached over the gearshift and caressed his nape. She ruffled his hair. A station wagon delivering Sunday newspapers slowed their progress up the coastal road. Soon Lemming Bay emerged between the poplars, glistening in the morning light. Koestler explained how the inlet had acquired its name from its deceptive calm—how ships had led one another into the treacherous narrows like lemming plunging from ice floes. And Joyce listened. That was his girlfriend's most attractive quality, more compelling than her naughty eyes and taut calves. For all of her quips and barbs, she had a golden ear. Eleanor had tussled through three oncologists before she'd settled on Joyce.

"I almost became a poet myself, you know," said Koestler.

"I'm glad you didn't," said Joyce, "or I'd be paying for the inn."

"I'm serious. I'm not saying that I had talent—I probably didn't have anything more than a poetic sensibility—but I did have yearnings." He did not mention the rejection letters that came with these yearnings, dozens from literary journals long defunct. He voiced none of the torment that came with accepting management of the family's struggling enterprise from his uncles. "I didn't come into this world whole cloth as a packaging manufacturer," he said.

Joyce's lips flickered with amusement.

"What's so funny?" demanded Koestler.

"I'm trying to picture you as a forlorn poet," she answered. "Don't take that the wrong way," she added. "I think it's rather endearing."

Koestler's spine stiffened. He swerved to avoid something swift and mammalian crossing the asphalt; for an instant, the tires yielded their traction. Traffic, to his surprise, proved dense and slow moving—a phalanx of pickup trucks and large American vehicles with bumper stickers advocating for Jesus and right whales. "How about you? Did you ever dream of becoming something other than an oncologist?"

"That's a question only a man could ask," said Joyce. "You can't imagine how hard it was for me to become a doctor. Who had time for pipe dreams?"

Now he bristled. The implication that his poetic ambitions had been pipe dreams stung with unnecessary truth. And yet he admired Joyce's candor—such a contrast to the subtleties and unspoken reproofs that had characterized his later years with Eleanor. He suppressed an instinct to defend himself. Soon they rounded a curve that exposed the cosmic scope of the bay. Low-slung fog half-concealed the mansions on the opposite promontory, yet the breaking surf remained as majestic as it had been in Koestler's youth.

"All vistas are the same," he quoted. "All cab rides. All funerals too. Yet no man concedes this uniformity while savoring the view or mourning his beloved."

He contemplated pulling off at a scenic overlook but pressed onward— hoping they might yet find themselves alone at the cenotaph. He also felt a vague urge to urinate.

"Your Bostwick was a cheery fellow, wasn't he?" asked Joyce.

Koestler did not have a chance to answer. An arrow pointing toward the entrance to Lemming Bay State Park poked from the undergrowth. Below the wooden marker flapped a vinyl banner: Ye Olde Medieval Fair & Lobster Festival. An identical threat appeared fifty years farther up the coastal road, its orange letters gothic and hostile. "A lobster festival," chimed Joyce. "I suppose it's festive for everyone except the lobsters."

Koestler rode the bumper of the jalopy in front of them, anticipating the desecration ahead. When he turned into the parking lot, an official in a rain parka was directing traffic. A titanic standard, suspended between two oaks, warned: "Welcome All, Unless You're Crabby or Shellfish." Beyond that hunkered stalls vending maritime fauna, and a triad of pillories in various sizes, and an enormous rubber shrimp wearing a lobster bib. The gathering discharged a stench of gutted porgies and moribund crustaceans.

"How exciting," Joyce declared. "I've always adored carnivals."

Koestler parked the Oldsmobile on a gravel knoll. He glanced at his watch—8:45—and already the lot stood more than half full. A bejowled "peddler" decked out in lime tunic and waist-length maroon cape approached them, hawking "saintly relics" from a leather pouch for "fifty ducats" a bone. Koestler led Joyce away by the hand. Wishing that none of these benighted nitwits had yet made it up the trail to the cenotaph was not realistic, of course, yet still he hoped that a solitary moment for proposing might be possible.

"Oh, look!" cried Joyce. "An execution."

An execution, indeed! In the clearing leading up to the trailhead stood what appeared to be a gimcrack gallows, surrounded by a sea of aluminum folding chairs. All of the chairs were white and square-backed in matrimonial style, yet they reminded Koestler of the World War I graves he'd seen at the British cemetery in Ypres. Most sat unoccupied, coated with dew. A pair of knights armed with poleaxes called for attention and motley-capped jester blew a bugle. Then a cassocked dignitary, Mayor Tuck, read a scroll that condemned several absent witches for their notorious sorcery. What they were actually witnessing, Koestler realized after a moment, was dress rehearsal for a mock hanging that was scheduled for later that day.

"You may buy these women freedom, my friends," proclaimed the ersatz mayor. "But it will cost you dearly." The proceeds funded college tuition for the children of disabled lobstermen; the highest bidders won all-you-can-eat suppers at a local surf and turf joint.

Koestler tugged gently at Joyce's hand. "A cenotaph is beckoning us," he coaxed.

"We wouldn't want to keep poor Bostwick waiting," said Joyce.

Yet they'd no sooner escaped the execution when Joyce caught sight of the pillories and asked him to snap her photo posing in confinement. "Jill will get a kick out of this," she said. "Are you sure you don't want one for your daughters?" After that, she insisted on sampling the chowder, steaming from a nearby cauldron. "You don't mind, do you?" she asked—seeking permission like a child. How could he deny her? So he sat opposite her at a wooden table while she ate, his eyes darting intermittently to his wristwatch and to the line outside the port-o-john. His frustration mounted. All around them swarmed merchants in medieval garb and rotund tourists corralling children. An entire family costumed as bivalves, headed by Papa Scallop, handed out flyers for half-day excursions to local barrier islands. When the mock execution concluded, a pair of lute-wielding troubadours performed from the same platform.

"Okay," said Joyce, wiping her lips with a napkin. "I've done my part for the local economy. Now let's pay our respects to Mr. Bostwick."

Koestler reached into his pocket, confirming the presence of the ring. The truth was that a part of him no longer wanted to visit the cenotaph—a part of him, to be honest, wanted to return home. But if he didn't propose to Joyce here, he knew, he wouldn't propose to her anywhere, so he locked his fingers around hers and led her up the footpath.

"On the way back," said Joyce, "I want to get something for Mama. And also for my cousin, Jackie, in Tallahassee."

He let her talk about her cousin, a retired hair stylist who'd lost three toes to diabetes. After high school, Joyce and Jackie had worked side by side as concessioners at Coney Island. Later, they'd taken their daughters together to Disney World. Koestler found that he didn't give a damn about Jackie Silverberg and her health problems. Not one iota. What he really wanted was to get the entire proposal business over and done with so that he might use the lavatory.

They climbed a rise to the sight of the granite cenotaph.

A pair of teenage girls tossed a Frisbee in the adjacent meadow, but otherwise the landscape appeared surprisingly pristine. No human seashells. No medieval monks. And yet the monument itself struck Koestler as smaller than he'd remembered, somehow diminished. The magnolias had vanished—not even stumps remained; in their place, a small plaque commemorated their loss to fungal blight. The gray stone appeared stark and naked.

Koestler steered Joyce to the far side of the memorial, where the cenotaph quoted a couplet from *Diphtheria*. On the return from his previous visit, he recalled, he'd argued with Bud Scheuer about the selection of verses chosen for engraving.

"I suppose the crowds arrive after lunch," quipped Joyce. "In any case, I am glad you brought me here. It *is* a beautiful view."

Koestler had hardly glanced out at the bay, which rolled away toward the ocean like a giant maw. Intense pulsations throbbed his carotids; his hand clutched the ring case inside the pocket of his trousers. How different this moment was than the one he had envisioned. He retrieved the plush case and held it open toward Joyce. "Will you marry me?" he asked.

"Mart?" asked Joyce. "Are you . . . ?"

"I am," he said. "Please say yes."

Joyce did not say yes. Instead, for an instant, she wore an unmistakable if only loosely untranslatable expression—one that said something like, *Why did you have to go ahead and ruin everything?* "That's a lot to think about," she said.

"I love you," said Koestler—already defeated. "Say yes now and we'll do the thinking later."

She took his arm and wrapped it around her slender waist. But she offered neither a yes nor a no—until she'd yielded the possibility of either.

And so hope led to disappointment and then to unvoiced anger. On the ride home the following afternoon, they spoke of small matters: her mother's glaucoma, his daughter's new boyfriend, whether they would attend an upcoming benefit bruncheon at St. Dymphna's. Koestler deposited her at her apartment, pecking her on the lips, and pledged to call the next day. Yet he returned from work that evening exhausted and cross, and soon three days had elapsed, and then two weeks, and then a full month without a phone call. Marriage was a matter of tradeoffs, he reminded himself, and soon the costs, economic and emotional, eclipsed the benefits.

Six months later, a mutual friend informed him of Bud Scheuer's latest divorce. "Poor sop," Koestler replied, grateful that his own matrimonial inclinations lay solidly behind him. He said nothing of the descent from Lemming Bay, of the thirty-minute hike down from the cenotaph to the festival, where they had arrived in time for the jousting demonstration, nothing of the searing white heat that coursed up his arm and into his chest as he contemplated the ring inside the case, clasped between his tremulous fingers.

THE AMAZING MR. MORALITY

—⟪◦⟫—

I

One of life's great enigmas was that an idea so colossally misguided could come from the mouth of a woman so stunningly beautiful. That mouth—with its adorable gap between the two front teeth—belonged to Erica Sucram, editor-in-chief of Hager Crossing's weekly newspaper, *The Double Crosser*, and the idea was for Grossbard to pen a regular column in which he answered ethical questions from readers.

Among the arguments against the plan was that Grossbard didn't know the first thing about ethics—he didn't even consider himself a particularly ethical person—and he hadn't written anything since college, unless one counted an occasional case report published in a psychiatric journal. Another objection was that fifteen years had done nothing to diminish his high school crush on the auburn-haired editor, a woman now married—happily, it appeared—to a broad-shouldered blowhard who infuriated Grossbard to the tips of his ears. Add to that the fact that he only planned to remain in Hager Crossing for a few months, and that he was unreliable by nature, as well as somewhat lazy, and Ted Grossbard couldn't conceive of any justifiable reason to assume the role of "Mr. Morality." Especially not for 16,000 hapless souls who, unlike himself, hadn't yet had the sense to escape a sleepy Philadelphia suburb best known for its annual Quince Pudding Festival.

But Erica had asked him. And she was still dazzling. And he remained an idiot—at least where women were concerned. Only this combination could explain how he'd come to be seated in a vacant conference room on the sixth floor of the Hay & Halstead Building, from which *The Double Crosser*'s staff kept a wary watch over the town, contemplating a letter that asked, *If you're going to commit a murder, is it worse to kill when the victim is sleeping or awake? (PS: This is a serious question.)*

He'd separated the readers' questions—of which dozens had arrived during the course of only seven days—into three stacks. One pile contained letters and printed email messages that sought advice, but did not raise genuine issues of right vs. wrong: *Can I sue my daughter's pediatrician and still play tennis with his wife? Do I owe it to my husband to visit a marriage counselor before I file for divorce?* And his favorite, handwritten in pink on lined notebook paper: *How many sex partners does it take to become "promiscuous"?* In a second pile, he placed the run-of-the-mill moral challenges of the sort that he'd anticipated when they'd launched the column, questions in line with those Erica had fabricated for their first installment the previous week: *My employer fired me unfairly, but accidentally paid me overtime for a shift I didn't work. Do I have to return the money?* The third set of letters, which Grossbard reread with increasing gloom, posed quandaries that seemed to spring from the minds of sociopaths. Even his four years as a psychiatry resident at one of New York City's busiest public hospitals hadn't prepared him for this much unvarnished evil: *I've discovered that my sister's husband is cheating on her; when I tell her, is it reasonable to expect her to compensate me for the information?* And *My aunt plans to leave me $10,000 in her will to look after her dog; is it okay if I drop the animal off at a shelter after she dies and use the cash to help pay for my kid's college tuition (a better use, in my opinion)?* And *Is it wrong to remove a demented relative from life support before Jan 1 to avoid adverse changes in the tax code?* Grossbard held out hope that a few of these dilemmas might be pranks—but certainly not all of them.

A rap on the door jolted him from his despair. Moments later, Erica entered the conference room, carrying a steaming beverage. Grossbard was about to thank her for the coffee, when she took a sip from the cup. "Any progress?" she asked.

"The best ones," he replied, "are those that have absolutely *nothing* to do with ethics. As though I'm the 'Answer Man' or something. Here's my favorite: *Is it true that actress Deanna Durbin left movies because she's afraid of germs?* What's unfathomable is that somebody cared enough to ask."

Erica peered through the Venetian blinds, then returned to the conference table and set down her cup. "I really appreciate you doing this."

"You may not appreciate the questions I've chosen," he said.

"I'm sure they'll be fine. Like I told you, the purpose of this column is to generate interest, and if that means stirring up controversy, so be it."

The purpose of this column, reflected Grossbard, is for me to indulge the momentary delusion that if I spend enough time with you over the next few months, I'll be able to lure you away from that glad-handing husband of yours. Deep down, he suspected he'd have to settle for something far less: an opportunity to mock the people he'd grown up around without their realizing it.

"Can I help at all?" asked Erica.

Grossbard shook his head. He wondered at what age—if ever—he'd lose his desire for her. Seventy? Ninety? Or maybe she'd always be branded indelibly upon the romantic lobe of his brain as the dreamy sixteen-year-old girl who'd told him he was "too smart" for her and then proved it by dating a hockey player.

"Okay, I'll let you work. Just get me something by four o'clock."

So Grossbard opened his laptop and started typing:

Intuitively, killing a person as he sleeps might seem more ethical, since it would likely cause that person less suffering. On the other hand, the victim would lose a chance to make a final statement while dying, and possibly an opportunity to clear his conscience before God, which still matters to some individuals. Moreover, if vengeance were one's principal motive, then a case could be made that giving the victim an instant to recognize that he is going to perish, and why, achieves a higher degree of justice. . . .

His goal was to keep his responses as ambiguous as possible.

II

Erica pitched the idea at the municipal dump. Grossbard had returned home to clean out his mother's house. After her death in May—she'd tripped going down the kitchen stairs and hit her head on the cellar door—he'd spent just enough time in Hager Crossing to arrange her affairs, then returned to Manhattan to complete his psychiatric training. His full-time job at the state hospital wasn't slated to begin until September, which now afforded him two months to undo his mother's four decades of packrattery. That was how he ended up at the town's household waste facility, on a sweltering July afternoon, pitching rope-bound bundles of *National Geographic* onto a fifty-foot mound of discarded paper. The air around him smelled like a giant Kleenex box.

A pickup truck came jouncing along the gravel service road and the driver backed the vehicle directly against the tower of papers. The truck bed housed a similar tower in miniature, noted Grossbard—pyramids of newspapers held in brown grocery bags. When a young woman emerged from the cab, he first registered her flawlessly curved figure. Several seconds elapsed before he recognized the woman behind the cotton dress and sunglasses as the enchanting Erica Sucram.

Grossbard hadn't seen Erica since his five-year high school reunion, when she'd hugged him as though she thought of him daily—and then promptly ignored him. He had, however, kept track of her progress through life via occasional Internet searches, usually conducted in the aftermath of his own failed relationships. He knew that she'd married and that she'd assumed management of the newspaper when her father, who'd served as both editor and publisher for forty years, retired to Arizona. Grossbard's initial instinct wasn't to approach her, as a sane person might, but to hide.

And then she removed her sunglasses and said his name.

"Teddy Grossbard," she said again. "As I live and breathe."

"I'm *Ted* now," he replied.

"Unbelievable. Really." Erica returned her sunglasses back to their perch; they were the reflective variety, which prevented Grossbard from seeing her eyes—and left him feeling defenseless. "I was just telling Palmer that we needed someone absolutely brilliant for our new ethics columnist— and now I run into you after all these years. Amazing."

"I'm only in town for a few months. Mopping up after my mother."

"I heard. I'm sorry," said Erica. "In any case, since you are here, I intend to take full advantage of the opportunity."

She tried to sell him on the ethics Q & A as a local version of a similar column running in the *New York Times*. She was also adding new features on cooking, financial planning, and relationships. "I want to include a sex advice column too," she said, "but Palmer's afraid it might tarnish our image." The impetus for these moves, Grossbard learned at the end of her pitch, was that, for the first time in its ninety-eight-year history, *The Double Crosser* faced competition. The *Laurendale Ledger*, a daily in the neighboring town, had started covering the news of Hager Crossing at www. CrossConnect.com. "To be honest, Ted," said Erica, "there isn't enough straight news here to go around."

"I don't know the first thing about ethics," Grossbard protested.

"They won't know that. You're a doctor, right? Well, if you wear a white coat around the hospital, that's enough for people to trust that you know what you're taking about."

"But I *do* know what I'm talking about at the hospital . . . because I *am* a doctor."

"I'm just using that as an analogy. Anyway, you were always brilliant. We'll give you an impressive title and people will think you're an expert." Erica's phone rang; she glanced down at the caller's number but did not answer. "It's also likely that once you get the hang of it, you'll actually develop some genuine expertise."

"You really want me to bill myself as Dr. Grossbard, Professional Ethicist?"

"Lord no! Not 'Dr. Grossbard.' That makes you sound like the villain from some science fiction movie," said Erica—ignoring the fact that it was actually his name. "I was thinking, 'Mr. Morality.' Nice and simple."

"You can't mean that. 'Mr. Morality'? Why not, 'The Amazing Mr. Morality'?"

He'd been jesting, but she weighed his suggestion seriously. "Shorter is better. Anything with 'amazing' in it makes you sound like a magician."

That was the first thing she'd said that actually made any sense. Grossbard lifted a bag of *National Geographics* from the trunk of his mother's Plymouth. "I really appreciate the offer," he said. "That being said, I don't think I'm the right person."

"But you are. I'm sure of it," said Erica—in a voice at once desperate and demanding. "Please, Ted. For me. For old times. Give it a trial run."

And before he knew it, he was trailing Erica's pickup back to the Hay & Halstead Building to meet with her husband.

III

Erica's husband, Palmer Quall, had taken over the business side of the newspaper from her father. What had actually happened, Grossbard later learned from Alyssa, the loose-tongued receptionist, was that Quall had failed the Pennsylvania bar exam on his third attempt, and the white-shoe Philadelphia law firm where he'd been an associate lost patience with him right around the same time that his father-in-law decided to retire. That didn't prevent Quall from hanging his law diploma on his office wall, or signing his name Palmer G. Quall, Esq., which was technically legal in New Jersey. He greeted his wife's "childhood friend" with a handshake forceful enough to spin a slot machine. To Grossbard, the man's sharp jaw and stocky build recalled the long-gone hockey player.

"I've recruited Ted for our ethics column," said Erica. "He's a very successful psychiatrist in New York City."

Nothing could have been further from the truth—he hadn't even passed his national board exams yet—but he'd learned not to challenge someone in the process of embellishing his credentials.

"Grossbard. Grossbard," said Quall, after Erica had left them alone in the publisher's office. "I can't tell you how often my wife mentions you. Smart guy, she says. First-rate fellow."

It was hard to imagine Erica referring to anyone as a "first-rate fellow."

"So you're a headshrinker," said Quall. "Impressive. I seriously considered becoming a physician myself, you know." His remark carried a dismissive undertone, as though entering medicine was as easy as ordering a different entrée in a restaurant. "Of course, I would have chosen a more hands-on specialty. Probably neurosurgery. If you're going to tamper with brains, I say, you might as well fix them."

Grossbard had been prepared to give Erica's husband the benefit of the doubt; the doubt had now triumphed. "If you do decide you want to go to medical school, let me know," he offered. "Maybe I can help."

"Very generous of you, Teddy," replied Quall. "But I'm going to stick to lawyering for now. Lawyering and publishing are both full-time jobs." Erica's husband leaned back in his chair, his arms clasped behind his neck, and for an instant Grossbard feared he might rest his feet on the desktop. "Glad to have you on board," he said. "Let's get all of the business talk out of the way, and then we can chat."

Quall proceeded to outline the terms of his contract. The whole enterprise seemed excessively formal to Grossbard—especially the clauses on international syndication rights—but he didn't care enough to object. What nearly set him off was the pay scale. Fifty dollars per column. That was a fraction of how much he could earn seeing a single psychiatric patient. Even Medicaid paid more. His indignation had nothing to do with the money itself. Until Quall had mentioned reimbursement, he'd assumed he'd be writing the column for free. Rather, what provoked him was the sense that his efforts could be bought and sold so cheaply.

"Fifty whole dollars," he remarked. "Astounding."

"We like to do right by our employees," said Quall. "Although I have to emphasize, for the record, that you're technically an independent contractor and not an employee of the newspaper."

Quall set the document on his desk blotter and Grossbard signed.

"Never sign anything without reading it," warned Erica's husband as he scooped up the paperwork. "You could have agreed to sell me a kidney, for all you know."

Grossbard kept his fingers entwined, his hands locked together on his lap, insurance against a sudden urge to strangle the man across the desk.

"You're lucky I'm an honest dealer," observed Quall. "In any event, I'm excited we'll be working together. You married?"

"Can't say that I am."

"Girlfriend?"

"Not yet," replied Grossbard.

"That's a healthy attitude. Not yet," said Quall. "No matter. I was going to invite your family out on our cabin cruiser—but you're welcome to come solo. It's my new toy. Thirty-four feet."

"I'm not a water person."

Erica's husband eyed Grossbard soberly. He appeared to be assessing whether Grossbard's words contained some hidden threat—but then he concluded that they were merely a joke. "I'm not a water person," he echoed, chuckling. "That's a good one."

"But I'm really not a water person," said Grossbard.

"You're too much," answered Quall. "Tell me you're not a water person after you've caught a forty-pound bluefish." Erica's husband then rose abruptly and shook Grossbard's hand, signaling the close of their meeting.

In the corridor that connected Quall's office to both the newsroom and the reception desk—its walls lined with framed front pages of vintage *Double Crossers*—Grossbard ran into Erica. "How was Palmer?" she asked. "He's not that bad, is he?" It struck Grossbard as a strange question to raise about one's own husband, especially if one were sure of the relationship, so although Erica seemed otherwise content with the good-looking imbecile, this question gave the young psychiatrist hope.

IV

The task of emptying his mother's house—his own boyhood home— proved daunting beyond what even Grossbard had anticipated. The truth of the matter was that his mother had been more of a full-blown hoarder than a pack rat. While nothing on the premises could be classified outright as junk, many of the items that clogged the rooms from floor to ceiling, preventing easy egress, offered limited utility. A retired suburban math teacher simply didn't require thirty-two umbrellas or a carton of Walter Mondale campaign literature. Grossbard told himself that he hadn't realized how bad matters had become, but the reality was that, deep down, he had known all along—he'd simply chosen to look the other way until it was too late—and this led to an unhealthy dose of guilt that compounded his already considerable grief. Although his father resided in Alaska with his third wife, and although Victor Grossbard sent a mass greeting every New Year's, and a card on his son's birthday, the death of Grossbard's mother left him feeling like an orphan.

Except for the few hours each morning when he dropped in at the newspaper office—more for an excuse to interact with Erica than out of journalistic necessity—he spent most of his time sorting through the vestiges of his mother's illness. In what had once been her son's childhood bedroom, Sue Grossbard had stored sacks of diatomaceous earth, shopping bags full of wool sweaters, milk cartons brimming with large-print mystery novels. As Grossbard emptied the house, he couldn't help thinking that, soon enough, another family would move into the split-level at 120 Steinhoff Street, bringing its own cares and aspirations and offspring, and that no trace of his own boyhood would remain. The prospect made him tear up, even though, as a psychiatrist, he knew his response to be irrational. Children become adults; real estate changes hands. That is the way of the world. Yet, on impulse, he took a permanent magic marker and, in the master bedroom, scrawled "Sue Grossbard called this home from 1972 to 2012" across the unpainted back of the sliding closet door.

As much as the house depressed Grossbard, the town depressed him more. Hager Crossing was a commuter suburb. Doctors and bankers sent their children to the community's nationally ranked schools, then dispatched those same offspring to top-tier colleges and relocated to avoid the property taxes. As a result, few of Grossbard's boyhood friends stuck around. To the people who did recognize him on his forays into the commercial district—an ageless waitress at the Star Crossed Café and his retired kindergarten teacher, Mrs. Montcrief—he remained bucktoothed Teddy Grossbard, the awkward, earnest teenager with the dental deficiencies. Three years of orthodontics during college had done little to reshape their memories. The only exception was his mother's elderly and somewhat unhinged neighbor, Mr. Berg, who approached Grossbard one afternoon while the psychiatrist knelt in the garage, sorting through gardening implements, and said, "Glad you got those awful fangs fixed, Theodore. You actually look like a normal human being now."

But then something peculiar happened. Grossbard had driven to the village library, hoping to donate his mother's mystery novels, and he found himself parking alongside Penny Claypool, whose daughter had been a year behind him in elementary school, and who'd become a local celebrity, if such a thing existed, for winning the Quince Pudding-Off eleven years in a row. Claypool wore a plaster boot on one foot and limped, assisted by a metal cane. The makeup on her face glistened like an oil sheen. In his entire life, Grossbard had probably exchanged a dozen sentences with the woman—at inter-class picnics and end-of-year musicals—but now she greeted him as though she'd spent years patiently awaiting his return to town.

"Teddy Grossbard," she declared—invading his personal space. "I wanted you to know that I just love your new morality column. Horace does too. We even clipped it out and mailed it to Veronica in Seattle."

"Thank you," said Grossbard.

The plan had been for him to pen the column anonymously, but Grossbard soon learned that nothing at *The Double Crosser* remained out of public view for long while Alyssa staffed the front desk. In spite of Claypool's praise, the psychiatrist found his unmasking to be upsetting. Wouldn't people think him a pompous ass for calling himself Mr. Morality and doling out wisdom leagues above his pay grade?

"Best thing in the whole darn paper," said Claypool, tapping her cane on the asphalt for emphasis. "I told Veronica, if I ever become demented, and she can cheat the taxman by pulling the plug on me ahead of schedule, all the power to her."

Nor was Claypool's enthusiasm a fluke. The next morning, while Grossbard was depositing unworn bathrobes at the Goodwill Center, a complete stranger complimented him on his journalistic efforts. "I looked you up on Google," said the woman, a stout sixty-something matron whose lipstick matched her obvious wig. "You raised several excellent points in that column of yours. Personally, I've never understood how people can spend so much money on pets while children are starving." That same afternoon, he received no less than three email messages complimenting his work.

Yet the most surprising encounter was with Mr. Berg, his mother's neighbor, who'd been an odd duck as long as Grossbard remembered him. The man had shared his dwelling with an equally odd younger sister when Grossbard was growing up, but in her fifties, the strange woman had converted to Catholicism and joined a Carmelite convent. She'd sent Grossbard's mother a card each Easter, containing hash marks for every Chaplet of St. Michael she'd prayed on behalf of her former neighbor.

"I read your column," said Berg, surprising Grossbard as he rolled up his mother's surplus garden hoses. "It was okay. Not as interesting as the one online in the *Ledger*, if you want to know the truth. But okay."

And that was how Grossbard discovered that the *Laurendale Ledger* had also arranged for an ethics columnist to answer questions at www. CrossConnect.com.

V

At first, Grossbard was merely curious. Since he'd agreed to write his own column on a whim, and with considerable ambivalence, the idea that someone else had entered the local ethics business didn't particularly trouble him. In fact, when he logged onto the *Laurendale Ledger*'s web page that evening—a site far more polished than *The Double Crosser*'s—he'd initially hoped to glean some pointers from the competition. All of his indifference evaporated when, immediately below the heading, "Ask Dr. Ethics," he spotted the name Lester Findlay. To his horror, he found the same odious name atop the CrossConnect masthead, where Dr. Ethics was also listed as Senior Editor. Only the late hour kept him from driving into Laurendale on impulse and taking a swing at his rival ethicist, who happened to be the least ethical human being he'd ever met.

Findlay had been the first man to date Sue Grossbard after her breakup. He'd also been the process server who'd slapped her with the divorce papers. According to the version of the story Sue Grossbard repeated at social gatherings after she'd been supplanted by another fresh divorcée, speaking with equal parts venom and self-reproach, Findlay had actually begun his courtship with the line, "Now that you're single . . . "

Grossbard was twelve at the time, enduring an awkward transition from happy-go-lucky schoolboy to odd-looking adolescent. He suspected that Findlay, who in addition to being a moral Neanderthal also claimed the distinction of being the cheapest person he'd ever encountered, lurked behind his mother's decision not to invest in orthodontics—although he could never have proven this accusation in a court of law. What he did know for certain was that the man had cost his mother a small fortune in unpromising investments: emu farming, cadmium futures, kangaroo meat, a pawn-and-check-cashing enterprise that Findlay bankrupted in a matter of months. For the three years he dated Grossbard's mother, he'd been constantly on the make. The highlight in Grossbard's memory was when, instead of buying his girlfriend's son a gift for his thirteenth birthday,

Findlay had placed an arm on his shoulder and offered him a piece of "valuable" advice "worth more than any damn present": *Cheat the other guy before he cheats you.* Cheating had been the man's strong suit, Grossbard's mother later discovered—when he gave her a venereal infection that spread to her kidneys. And now the same degenerate who'd driven his mother into acute renal failure had repackaged himself as an authority on ethical living.

Findlay's first column enraged Grossbard further. His enemy had filched *The Double Crosser's* questions, dumbed them down, and provided reductive, sanctimonious answers of the sort one might find in a child's catechism. So on the subject of life support and taxation, a CrossConnect "reader" asked: *I'll inherit more money if my grandfather dies sooner. Can I pull the plug on him?* In response, Dr. Ethics had written: *Pulling the plug on your grandfather, or anybody else, is always wrong. People are not vacuum cleaners.* Grossbard found it galling that a complex moral question—on which he'd expended five-hundred words, while holding many more in reserve—had been reduced to meaningless simplicity by his nemesis. With regard to caring for a relative's dog, Findlay expounded: *Sacrificing your grandmother's dog to pay for your child's education isn't only wrong, it's stupid. Dogs are loyal. The moment your children leave for college, they forget you exist.*

VI

Grossbard arrived at *The Double Dealer's* office at nine o'clock the next morning, armed with a printout of Findlay's ripped-off column. Alyssa greeted him from behind the reception desk—and, in her furtive style, pumped him for gossip. He'd already learned the hard way to watch what he shared.

"You'd have made an excellent reporter," he replied. "But I don't have any secrets for you. Not today. Is Erica in yet?"

Alyssa took his rebuff in stride. "She's been here since 8:15. Staff meeting," said the receptionist. "You're staff now, Dr. Grossbard, aren't you? I suppose you're welcome to join them. They're in the main confer-ence room." Grossbard didn't mention that he was technically an independent contractor.

He followed the corridor lined with historic headlines toward the news desks, but halted in front of the glass-paneled meeting room. By now, Grossbard recognized all of the paper's employees: seven journalists, two volunteer photographers, and an assortment of advertising personnel. Erica sat at the far end of the conference table, scribbling furiously in a notebook. Chairing the assemblage was Palmer Quall, who caught sight of Grossbard and immediately beckoned him inside.

"Perfect timing, buddy," declared Quall. "I was just telling our team how excited we are about our new columnists. You're doing ethics, right?"

Grossbard found himself standing at the front of the room—the target of three dozen suspicious eyes. "So it seems," he agreed.

"Just checking," replied the publisher. "I'd hate to get you confused with the gal who offers those dating tips." Quall laughed at his own quip, a deep, somewhat hostile bellow of a laugh. "Any ethics wisdom for your colleagues?"

Grossbard was tempted to say, *Cheat the other guy before he cheats you.* Yet he suspected his boss—and Quall, in principle, was his boss—already had this particular precept down pat. "I charge good money for ethics advice," he finally answered, hoping to deflect the inquiry.

"And we pay you good money," rejoined Quall. "Now show us what we're getting for our buck."

So the imbecile wanted him to perform like a seal. What made matters worse, Quall didn't even realize how offensive his request was. All that kept Grossbard from resigning on the spot was a pointed glance from Erica—a glance that begged for patience.

"I'll tell you one thing that's unethical," said Grossbard. He deposited Findlay's columns on the tabletop like People's Exhibit A. "Stealing some-one's intellectual property. Have you read that so-called ethics column on the *Ledger* website? I'm ready to sue the pants off that bastard, Findlay, if you are."

"There you have it," said Quall. "Words of wisdom."

"I'm dead serious," persisted Grossbard.

Erica cleared her throat. "We can talk about this later, Ted."

The strain in her voice kept Grossbard from objecting. And then Quall delivered a few more empty remarks regarding the quality of various features and the importance of teamwork before he adjourned the meeting.

VII

"So what was that all about?" Grossbard asked Erica.

They'd stepped up the block to the Star-Crossed Café for an early lunch. The coffee nook hadn't changed in decades: the same paintings of mermaids and starfish graced the walls, the same one-armed proprietor managed the cash register. Both waitresses, one heavyset, the other bony, shouted orders as though commanding artillery. Grossbard had been with Erica to the café numerous times in high school, always with packs of mutual friends, but now—as absurd as he knew it to be—he found himself genuinely somewhat awed to find himself alone with her at their one-time hangout.

"You mean Palmer? He doesn't like distractions at staff meetings," said Erica. "Sorry about that. I just sensed things might go south."

"I see. It must be hard to walk on eggshells all the time."

Erica poured sugar into her tea. "It's not so bad. It isn't like Palmer's going to hit anybody—he just gets a bit worked up." She cradled the cup in her palms and gazed absently into the ether. "The worst he's ever done was to make a few idle threats—but he was provoked."

"Idle threats?"

"You'd have been proud of him. He told your friend Lester Findlay that if the guy didn't stop poaching story ideas from us, he'd burn his office to the ground."

That certainly did earn Quall points in Grossbard's book. Nonetheless, it boggled his mind that his crush had married this dolt—but he had the sense not to say so.

"I realize you're not a fan of Palmer's," said Erica. "You have to trust me that he's a good guy, deep down. He's just a bit insecure. You don't know the half of what he's gone through." She sounded as though she were trying to persuade herself of the extenuating circumstances too. "I don't want to give you the wrong idea. My husband is one of the most loyal and devoted guys I've ever met. You'd be surprised how rare a quality like loyalty can be among eligible men."

"And he owns a cabin cruiser," jibed Grossbard. "Thirty-four feet."

"Don't be a jerk," snapped Erica.

"I'm just saying . . ."

"What's wrong with owning a boat?" demanded Erica. "You should come out with us on the bay sometime. It's actually a lot of fun." As she spoke, a perfect sweep of color filled her cheeks. "Anyway, let's talk about something else."

"What happened to that guy you dated in high school?" asked Grossbard. "The hockey player with no neck?"

"Todd Serspinksi? I have no clue," replied Erica. "Let me rephrase what I said. Can we please talk about something that has nothing to do with my romantic life?"

"Like my lawsuit against Lester Findlay?"

"Not going to happen. We've already checked with our attorneys," said Erica. "Apparently, you can't copyright ethics scenarios. As long as he doesn't steal the words themselves, we're shit out of luck."

"Unless I kill him."

"Agreed. Unless you kill him," said Erica. "But you won't do that. You're not the killing type."

"People change," said Grossbard—his statement loaded with meaning.

"Not that much, they don't."

As though to underscore Erica's point, the scrawny waitress appeared at that instant and slammed their plates down on the tabletop. Grossbard was suddenly too busy deciding which condiments he wanted with his sandwich to focus on any potential subtext in Erica's words. "Bon appétit," said Erica.

They sat in silence for a few seconds, sampling their meals. Then Erica leaned forward—and after glancing around the café—said in a near whisper, "We're getting slaughtered by Findlay, Ted. It's a total massacre."

"It can't be that bad," he offered.

"Beyond bad. We can barely make payroll. We still have the mom and pop accounts—for now—but the chain stores are asking why they should advertise with us when they can reach the same market at CrossConnect for a quarter of the price."

"They have a point there," conceded Grossbard. But he quickly shifted into therapist mode and asked, "But what's the worst thing that could happen?"

Erica looked as though she might sob. She'd displayed a few breakdowns of this sort in high school—including the night she told him he was "too smart" for her—yet her outbursts only managed to augment her sex appeal. Who wouldn't fall in love with a beautiful woman at her most vulnerable? "Honestly, Ted, I'm scared. If *The Double Crosser* fails, I don't have a Plan B—all I've ever done is run a newspaper." And then Erica was sobbing. "I'm sorry," she cried. "It's just—we were hoping to have a baby. And now instead of a successful businesswoman with a family, I'm going to have to beg money off my parents. It's so humiliating. If it gets bad enough, we might have to move to Arizona."

"Are you sure you don't want me to murder Findlay?"

"I never said I didn't want you to," said Erica, smiling through her tears. "All I said was that you didn't have it in you."

She wiped her cheeks with her napkin. If anything, the slight puff around her lids made her sloe eyes all the prettier.

"And, Ted, I want you to know how grateful I am that we've become friends again," said Erica. "Aren't you glad we didn't date in high school? That probably would have poisoned everything. Strange how things work out."

"Strange indeed," said Grossbard.

He wasn't sure what Erica's remarks meant for his current romantic prospects, although he thought about them for the remainder of the day. What their lunch had done was solidify his resolve to lure her away from her insufferable husband—although, for the moment, he had no idea how to accomplish that.

VIII

Years of psychiatric training had taught Grossbard that nothing good ever comes from direct confrontation with depravity. You might as well argue with a parking meter or a vending machine. That knowledge was not enough to keep him from driving out to Laurendale three days later to share a few choice words with Lester Findlay.

While the *Ledger* maintained a lavish office suite on the ground floor of an eighteenth-century tavern in the historic town center, a quick visit to that location revealed that CrossConnect didn't operate out of the paper's main headquarters. Rather—and this information cost Grossbard a pair of twenties—Findlay ran the satellite website from a trailer stationed behind his own home in downscale Camden Heights.

The structure itself was something of an eyesore, one of those low-slung, FEMA-style monstrosities used by construction crews, but it didn't stand out in a neglected, mixed-use neighborhood where half the dwellings were swathed in plywood. Findlay's house—a dispirited clapboard cube painted a drab olive—sagged between a funeral parlor and a freestanding pool hall. The telephone wires hung low enough to be reached with an outstretched arm. If Palmer Quall ever did burn the place to the ground, the psychiatrist reflected, he'd be doing the community a favor.

Grossbard found the trailer door propped wide open, an electrical fan whirring on the threshold. He climbed the cinder block steps and knocked on the metal siding. From the depths of the trailer rose the sound of a toilet flushing, followed by the emergence of Lester Findlay, tucking the tails of his shirt into his blue jeans as he approached. In Grossbard's memory, Findlay had been handsome and fit. The man standing before him, his eyes aglow with menace, carried a tire of flesh

above his belt, and his salt-and-pepper ponytail looked in desperate need
of washing. The cluttered workspace surrounding him appeared marginally sanitary, at best. Grossbard mused to himself that one match
could ignite the place rapidly.

"You want something?" demanded Findlay.

The conman shuffled to an iron desk strewn with manila folders, open
soda cans, and foil ashtrays crammed with cigarette butts.

"I'd like to discuss your column," said Grossbard.

"I don't hold office hours. This isn't some swanky college," retorted
Findlay. "Send me a letter and I might just answer. If I feel like it."

Grossbard had come braced to duel with the charismatic swindler
who'd hoodwinked his mother. Nothing had prepared him for the two
decades of wear that had transformed his nemesis into an irritable derelict.
Gone was the hail-fellow-well-met cheer that had once blinded Sue
Grossbard and irked her adolescent son. Life, the great equalizer, had
hewn Findlay down to size. Rather than pleasing Grossbard, the conman's
decline kindled his insecurities and led him to worry about his own future.

"You don't recognize me, do you?" he asked.

Findlay looked up, meeting him eye to eye for the first time. "Why
the hell should I recognize you?" And then a flash of insight struck the
man's face like a tidal wave, and a sneer crossed his lips. "Teddy Grossbard,"
he said. "You got yourself a set of fancy teeth." Findlay settled into the
swivel chair; its joints squealed under his weight. "I didn't know you still
lived around here."

"Don't fuck with me, Lester," warned Grossbard. "You damn well
know I'm writing an ethics column for *The Double Crosser*."

"Could be," replied Findlay, scratching his scalp. "Come to think of
it, I may have seen your byline. I guess that means I ought to congratulate
you."

Grossbard felt his temper rising. "What it means," he shot back, "is
that you'd better stop ripping off my columns."

An uncomfortable silence settled over the trailer, punctuated only by
the hum of the fan and the wail of a distant car alarm. Findlay reached

into the bottom drawer of his desk and for an instant Grossbard feared he might retrieve a handgun. Instead, he produced a bottle of aspirin and counted out three pills on his palm. "Imitation is the greatest form of flattery," said the conman, before popping the tablets into his mouth and chasing them down with the contents of a thermos. "If I were pinching your precious material, you should feel flattered."

"Well, I don't. Actually, I'm damn pissed."

Findlay smirked. "That's your choice, my boy. But it's not good for the old ticker." The conman pounded the left side of his chest with his fist. "I had myself two heart attacks getting pissed at people. No point in that. Now, I just get even."

"If you don't stop," said Grossbard, "you'll force me to take legal action."

His adversary remained unmoved. "I'd hate to see you do that, Teddy-boy. Any lawyer with an IQ over fifty could tell you that you'd be wasting your time. You can't copyright run-of-the-mill ethical dilemmas," he said. "So I suggest you take things in stride. It's just some friendly competition, after all—a custom of the industry, as they say. And besides, we're practically family."

This was too much for Grossbard. "We are *not* goddam family," he shouted. "I'd sooner die in the street than be related to you."

Findlay swatted the rejection away with his hand. "Suit yourself."

"My mother died in May, by the way. In case you care."

"I'm sincerely sorry to hear that," answered Findlay, oozing with false sympathy. "Fine gal, your mother. Great in the sack, too."

A decade earlier, Grossbard might have taken a swing at the man. But that was before years of psychotherapy, before he'd learned the power of restraint. So instead, he counted backwards from ten, glowering at Findlay all the while—knowing that a delayed response would upset the conman more than any lashing out. Then he turned on his heels and exited the overheated trailer without uttering a sound. From behind him, he heard the conman calling, "Chill out. I meant that as a compliment," but he let the words blow past him like so much unwanted hot air.

IX

Grossbard's encounter with Findlay proved surprisingly liberating. Now that the conman had insulted his dead mother, he felt no ethical obligation toward him whatsoever—not even the basic respect due a fellow human being. If he had been the killing type, he reflected, he'd have had no qualms about targeting the degenerate behind Ask Dr. Ethics. Instead, composing his column that afternoon, he couldn't resist taking a jab at the entire town of Hager Crossing. Let Findlay climb atop his high horse and dole out self-righteous bullshit. It would be far more entertaining, Grossbard decided, to tell the morally aberrant sinners of New Jersey exactly what they wanted to hear. After all, it seemed reasonable enough to assume that the majority of letters to Mr. Morality were seeking permission, not chastisement.

Grossbard had given up working at the offices of *The Double Crosser*. As much as he savored chatting with Erica, he dreaded encounters with Palmer Quall even more, and it was the publisher who often sought him out for meaningless conversation. Erica's husband was still determined to show Grossbard his motorboat; only by avoiding the man entirely could he hope to stave off the inevitable. So that afternoon, the psychiatrist settled down at the mahogany table in his mother's dining room—finally liberated from chandelier-high trash bags full of moth-eaten bedding and women's shoes—and dove into the stack of letters and printouts that contained the most outlandish reader questions.

Dear Mr. Morality, read one. *At a recent medical appointment, my doctor left her purse on the countertop in the examination room—and when she was called away to tend to another patient, I pocketed two hundred dollars in cash. I'm now worried that if she suspects me, it may impact our relationship in the future. How should I go about returning her money? Sincerely, Repentant on Rolleston Road.* By the end of the letter, Grossbard found himself grinning. The inquiry seemed ideally tailored for what he had in mind.

Dear Repentant, he wrote. *A fool and her money are soon parted. Do not let yourself be that fool. Your physician ought to know better than to leave her purse in a busy examination room. If she comes up a few dollars short, it should teach her a valuable lesson. As a doctor, she can afford the loss. In addition, she had a moral obligation to you, as her patient, not to tempt you in this manner. Since you are in possession of the money, and possession is nine tenths of the law, I strongly suggest you keep it. Call it a finder's fee. Put it to good use. Treat yourself to something indulgent. If you're truly afraid that this may compromise your healthcare in the future, consider firing your negligent physician and finding another one—preferably one more responsible with her money.*

Let Findlay top that.

Grossbard offered equally permissive answers to a lawyer contemplating an affair with his jailed client and a restaurant manager planning to bribe the county health inspector. Unlike his first round of answers, when he'd taken the responsibility seriously, Grossbard now enjoyed his assignment immensely, so much so that he lost track of the hour. By the time he'd finished committing his "wisdom" to paper, he'd already missed his four o'clock deadline. But that too struck him as fortuitous. Since Palmer Quall spent Friday evenings on his boat, preparing the cruiser for his celebrated Saturday excursions, Grossbard decided to deliver his Q & A to the newspaper office by hand in the hope of luring Erica out to dinner. If he'd missed her—and it was already past five o'clock—he could always slide his thumb drive under her door.

The Hay & Halstead Building stood opposite the railroad station, so Grossbard had to fight his way through battalions of commuters retrieving their cars. When he finally stepped off the elevator on the sixth floor, the lights in *The Double Dealer*'s office suite were off. To his surprise, the front door remained unlocked. Hoping he might catch Erica alone at her desk, he advanced through the darkened lobby and the lifeless newsroom. Unfortunately, the only office with light seeping around the edges of the doorframe belonged to Palmer Quall. Without warning, the publisher's door opened. Grossbard had just enough time to duck into the photocopying alcove.

Quall was speaking on his cell phone. "It should do the trick perfectly.

I can't thank you enough for sending it over," said the publisher. "That shit you buy in stores doesn't burn nearly as well." The conversation seemed innocent enough—Erica's husband might have been discussing propane for his barbecue grill—if not for his previous threats about burning Findlay's trailer to the ground. That earlier statement, coupled with the dire financial condition of *The Double Dealer*, made an innocent explanation less plausible.

As Grossbard registered the full significance of what he'd heard, his nostrils suddenly became aware of a pungent aroma rising over the background scent of copier fluid. It was unmistakable. Gasoline. He had his senses confirmed when Palmer Quall passed through the newsroom a moment later carrying two large rectangular canisters labeled PETROL. As soon as Grossbard heard the outer door shut behind Erica's husband, he rushed quickly to the conference room windows.

Six stories below, Palmer Quall strode to the corner of Pastarnack Place, opposite the festooned war memorial, and loaded the gasoline canisters into the trunk of his sports car. Grossbard struggled to keep his imagination in check. If one of his therapy patients had described what he'd just witnessed, Grossbard would have offered countless reasonable interpretations of the facts that did not involve arson. *You've watched too many movies*, he'd have said. Nonetheless, in his gut, Grossbard sensed that he'd diagnosed the case correctly: this imbecile who'd somehow married the woman of Grossbard's dreams was about to destroy the life of Lester Findlay, the person he despised most on the planet. And the best part of all was that Grossbard himself had no responsibility, moral or legal, for this scheme. All he had to do was watch and wait.

X

Over the ensuing weeks, as he went about the tedious business of preparing his mother's house for market, Grossbard played out a number of arson scenarios in his head. In his favorite, Quall botched the attack on Findlay's trailer and was easily apprehended by the police; after initially professing her loyalty, Erica recognized her husband's shortcomings and abandoned him for Grossbard, who'd strategically refused to criticize his romantic rival during the trial. Other permutations on the same theme involved Quall renouncing his wife for a heretofore unknown mistress who provided him an alibi in court, and even Quall dying amid the flaming folders of Findlay's office. In every version—and this is what mattered—Grossbard ended up married to Quall's wife.

The frustrating aspect of playing no role in Quall's plan was that Grossbard also had no means of accelerating it. As July drifted into August, his impatience intensified. Every morning, he logged onto his computer, hoping to find the CrossConnect website out of commission or a front-page news item reporting on the conflagration in the *Ledger*. Every morning, alas, he found himself sadly disappointed. Whatever Palmer Quall's intentions—and Grossbard remained confident that he'd assessed the situation accurately—the glad-handing publisher was not a man to be rushed.

Grossbard's only solace was the success of his column. To his amazement, his loose approach to ethics proved exactly in line with the tastes of the community. Soon enough, Ask Mr. Morality (they'd tweaked the title) earned a place as the most popular feature in the entire newspaper. Strangers left emotional messages on Grossbard's voicemail, thanking him for saving broken marriages, rescuing failing businesses, and liberating would-be transgressors "from the shackles of shame and guilt." He was even asked to deliver a lecture on self-forgiveness at the local Unitarian Church—although he had the good sense to decline the invitation.

He grew to relish his role in the moral undoing of Hager Crossing. He had limits, of course. Never did he condone outright depravity: murder or sexual assault or abuse of the truly vulnerable. On one occasion, he even referred a disturbing note from a would-be child molester to the authorities. In lower stakes matters, however, covering a wide swath of human deviance from larceny to adultery to robbing graves at a pet cemetery, he urged his neighbors to follow their worst instincts. They apparently did so—and showed their appreciation with offerings of wine and home-baked pies. Several small-time felons even attempted to share their loot, which *The Double Crosser* graciously accepted and then donated to charity. In Grossbard's battle with Lester Findlay for the moral center of the community, do-as-you-wish trounced do-as-I-tell-you. Only his peculiar neighbor, Mr. Berg, continued to prefer the shrill guidance of CrossConnect's Dr. Ethics.

Unfortunately, journalistic fame—even of the local variety—did not burn down a newspaper office or send a romantic rival to prison. In early August, however, another frustration arose to distract Grossbard temporality from his focus on the arson plot: Palmer Quall fixed him up on a date. The woman in question was Quall's cousin, Amanda, an event planner and would-be actress "working on her audition reel." Erica's husband broached the subject at the paper's summer picnic, which Erica had strong-armed Grossbard into attending.

"If she wasn't my cousin, *I'd* fuck her," Quall had confided.

"*And* if you weren't married," suggested Grossbard.

Erica's husband shot him a look of irritation. "Look, buddy, I'm doing you a favor. Chicks like this don't grow on trees." The publisher draped his arm over Grossbard's shoulder and walked him away from the crowd. It struck the psychiatrist that, with a quick jerk, the man could break his neck. "What's up with you?" asked Quall—and Grossbard detected a hint of suspicion, even paranoia, in his voice. "You don't have a secret girlfriend, do you? You're not holding out on me?"

So to avoid leaving the impression that he was having an affair with Erica, Grossbard agreed to join Quall on a fishing excursion with the man's cousin. It was unimaginable, he recognized, that he'd have any romantic interest in the event planner. The sad truth of the matter was that he didn't even enjoy events. But Quall and Erica quickly settled on the details of the outing, like lawyers negotiating a prison sentence, and Grossbard spent the subsequent week dreading the appointed Saturday morning. Initially, he'd prayed for rain, but when he mentioned the possibility, Quall informed him that the weather didn't matter. "Do you think the bluefish stay home on a cloudy day, Teddy? What kind of pansy are you?" Quall shook his head. "But have no fear, pal. We're going to make an angler out of you yet."

The fishing gods must have had the same intentions as Quall—or a perverse sense of humor—because a summer squall rode up the coast that weekend. Gale warnings covered Chesapeake Bay as far north at the Susquehanna River, but that didn't prevent Erica's husband from taking them out on the water. "I haven't sunk yet," he boasted as the four of them drove through the pounding rain to the marina. "Besides, that's why we carry life preservers."

"He's joking," Erica assured the event planner. "It's a very sturdy boat."

The event planner giggled. She was indeed very attractive, by conventional standards, although probably too slender for good health. As soon as they'd boarded the publisher's vessel, *The Magic Bullet*, Erica steered the pair of them into the cabin and did her utmost to facilitate a connection. That effort included serving the strongest bloody marys Grossbard had ever tasted. Meanwhile, Quall navigated the boat across the choppy inlet toward the open water.

"Didn't you tell me you had an ethics question for Ted?" asked Erica.

"Oh, I did, didn't I?" agreed the event planner. She turned to Grossbard and placed her hand on his forearm. "Here's the thing. I'm putting together my acting résumé—for the back of my headshot—and I'm wondering if I can get away with something. . . ."

"Get away ethically or get away practically?" asked Grossbard.

Amanda served up a blank smile. The distinction appeared to be lost on her.

"When I was in fifth grade," she continued, "my parents sent me to theater camp in New York City. The camp rented a studio on Broadway at 48th Street, and at the end of the summer, we staged *The Sound of Music* for our parents. I was Brigitta von Trapp."

The event planner flashed her teeth. Grossbard sensed that the performance had been one of the high points of the woman's life, but he held his tongue.

"What I'm wondering," said Amanda, "is whether I can write in my biographical sketch that I starred in *The Sound of Music* on Broadway."

The woman's question was so sincere, and so ludicrous, that Grossbard nearly spit out his drink. He caught Erica's eye over the event planner's shoulder, but she responded with an innocent smile. "That's an excellent question," she said. "Well, Mr. Morality? Can you help out a damsel in ethical distress?"

"Honestly," replied Grossbard. "That strikes me as a question for the competition. Our friend Findlay might have some wisdom for Amanda on the subject."

Amanda inquired who Findlay was, enabling Grossbard to shift the conversation to his ongoing rivalry with the conman. Since the event planner knew nothing about ethics or journalism and appeared to be generally slow on the uptake, Grossbard had essentially shut her out of the conversation.

"What I can't understand," he said to Erica, "is why a respectable newspaper like the *Laurendale Ledger* would hire a degenerate like that."

"Moola," she replied, rubbing her thumb against her fingertips. "To you, he's a degenerate. But on the phone with advertisers, the man's tongue is smooth as silk. He could persuade a tin-cup manufacturer into taking out print ads for the blind." Erica peered through a porthole into the storm and then clicked her cocktail glass against the event planner's drink. "Let's not talk shop," she said. "I'm sure Amanda doesn't care about Lester Findlay's sales technique."

"It's okay. I've always been interested in business," said Amanda. "If acting doesn't work out, I might become a talent agent."

"Let's hope acting works out," said Grossbard.

He hadn't meant his remark derisively—he'd intended to be supportive of her acting career—but somehow the words sounded wrong once they'd left his mouth. Since he couldn't think of anything else to say to his "date," he waited for her to speak, but she also remained silent, and an awkward hush enveloped the cabin. Even Erica appeared to be at a loss for words. Fortunately, Palmer Quall came barreling down the scuttle a moment later, his parka drenched, wearing a simultaneously tortured and enraptured expression that Grossbard had only seen once before: on the cover of *National Geographic*, in a photograph of a self-flagellating Filipino monk. "You'd better be enjoying yourself, Ted," he exclaimed. "Fresh surf. Hot women. I bet you never thought you'd have it this good!"

"Never," replied Grossbard.

Quall kissed Erica—hard, on the lips.

"I have more good news," said the publisher, addressing his wife. "That fuel my buddy sent over from Amsterdam. Smoothest burn I've ever experienced." Quall looked as though he'd struck oil in his vegetable patch. "So much for American diesel. From now on, it's only Holland's finest."

At first, Grossbard was far too unsettled by the kiss to absorb the publisher's preferences in fuel—which, in any case, seemed precisely the sort of insignificant nonsense that would interest a half-wit like Erica's husband. His rival has already moved on to discussing their fishing prospects when Grossbard registered the import of Quall's remarks. If the fuel in the man's trunk was for powering his boat, it obviously wasn't earmarked for burning down Findlay's office. So much for his fantasies of a whirlwind trial and rebound romance. Grossbard felt his mood sink rapidly, and as the vessel pitched against the breakers, nausea rose in his throat.

"Okay, enough gabbing," announced Quall. "Let's catch some fish."

He started to climb the scuttle, then stopped abruptly and returned to the cabin. "Wait. I forgot something," he said.

"Something important?" asked Erica.

"You tell me," he replied—and then he kissed her again. Not a couple-out-for-the-afternoon kind of kiss, but a Burt-Lancaster-Deborah-Kerr-*From-Here-To-Eternity* kiss that saw her heels leave the floor.

Amanda smiled at Grossbard, but looked away quickly. At that very moment, a particularly strong wave crashed against the side of the vessel, propelling the event planner toward him. She lost her footing and, on the way down, her shoulder collided with his abdomen. The blow, coming on top of his green gills, and probably exacerbated by Quall's display of affection, proved too much for Grossbard's system. When his date looked up at him from the deck, dazed and bloody, he vomited on her head.

XI

The fallout from the fishing expedition proved far less disastrous than Grossbard had initially feared. Amanda's injuries, while not serious, were enough to cut short their time on the bay, but Palmer Quall didn't appear too concerned: "It was lousy fishing weather anyway," he conceded. "But next time, Grossbard, use a bucket." He never mentioned the outing again, nor did he ever offer to fix up the psychiatrist on another unwanted date. To Grossbard's surprise, once it became clear that the event planner's only wounds were a bloody nose and a stained sweater, Erica readily acknowledged the humor in the situation. "Please don't repeat this to Palmer," she told him in the hospital lobby, while they waited for Amanda's discharge from the ER, "but I can't think of anyone more in need of a good dose of vomit." She squeezed his wrist and added, "There goes your chance to marry a Broadway star." They both burst into laughter simultaneously.

If there was a lasting downside to the excursion, it was the realization that Palmer Quall had no arson plot in the offing. This discovery knocked the wind, so to speak, out of Grossbard's sails. As the summer progressed, he'd sensed the tension in Erica's relationship with her husband, even detecting notes of outright regret, but never any concrete indication that she planned on leaving him. Only a drastic change was likely to overcome her inertia—and an arson arrest had been Grossbard's best hope. His only hope, in fact. Without the prospect of seducing Erica on the horizon, his days in New Jersey suddenly felt long and empty. Luckily, two unexpected events—one trivial, the other momentous—conspired to change Grossbard's outlook.

The minor event occurred five days after the fishing debacle, as Grossbard was contemplating how best to use his final weeks in Hager Crossing. He'd stopped by *The Double Crosser*'s office to retrieve the handful of letters that readers, possibly those too old for email and too cheap to pay for postage, tucked under the suite's front door. That morning, Alyssa had recovered only one note for him, but it proved fateful:

Dear Mr. Morality, I've been in conflict with my neighbor for years, and now he's started luring my dog, Ernie, to do its private business on his property, using exotic meats as bait. Then he videotapes Ernie in the act—and calls the dog warden, demanding that Ernie be put down as a nuisance. Once, when Ernie wouldn't take the bait, I even caught the bastard sprinkling feces on his own yard from a plastic bag. In short, my neighbor is trying to frame poor Ernie. What can I do to protect my rights, and my dog, and teach the bastard a lesson he'll never forget?

Not exactly an appropriate letter for Grossbard's column. Nonetheless, its contents were on his mind as he strolled up Pastarnack Place toward his parking spot, when a brassy voice hurled his name across the plaza. "Teddy! Hold up a moment." An instant later, he found himself in the company of Penny Claypool.

"Precisely the young man I was looking for," declared Claypool. She hugged him to her ample chest without warning, planting a moist kiss on his cheek and hitting his kneecap with her cane. "I just adore your column. I can't say that enough, can I? It's so straightforward. So honest."

"Thank you," replied Grossbard.

"I suppose you've heard the tragedy," she said. "We're all beside ourselves. It's just dreadful."

"What's happened?" asked Grossbard, feigning ignorance. "I've been out of town."

"You really don't know? Oh, it will come as such a shock." Claypool looked up and down the sidewalk as though on guard for spies. "Chester Kilsheimer was arrested. *Arrested!* It's just too awful."

Kilsheimer, a local restaurateur and booster, had served as grand marshal of the Quince Pudding Festival for decades. Between expressions of outrage and dismay, Claypool related that the businessman had been arrested for exposing himself behind the carousel at the county amusement park. "I'm sure it's all a terrible misunderstanding," insisted Claypool. "But that's neither here nor there. We still can't have the grand marshal of the Quince Pudding Festival accused—even unjustly accused—of flashing twelve-year-old boys. It just wouldn't do."

"I see what you mean," agreed Grossbard. "If you're looking for my official ethicist's opinion, I think it would be fine to tell Chester he can't serve this year."

Penny Claypool sighed. "I've already done that. But that leaves us without a grand marshal—and the festival starts next week."

A sinking feeling hit Grossbard's gut with the force of a depth charge.

"I've spoken with the board," she continued. "We all agree that we need a replacement of unimpeachable reputation—someone to divert attention away from . . . from unpleasantness. And I'm delighted to say our decision was unanimous, Teddy. We've appointed *you* the new grand marshal for this year's festival."

Penny Claypool beamed at him as though she'd offered him the English throne.

"I don't know what to say," he stammered.

"You don't have to say anything," said Claypool. "I imagine you're feeling overwhelmed at the moment—it's a great honor, but it's also a fearsome responsibility. Yet I want to assure you that we wouldn't offer you this position if we weren't confident that you were up to the task. Quite frankly, what you've done for the moral core of this town has been long overdue. You'll have our backing, come hell or high water."

"Unless I drop my trousers at an amusement park."

A look of alarm flared across Claypool's face—its horror intensified by her garish makeup. "We've agreed it's best to say as little as possible about certain matters," she said with forced dignity. "For the sake of the accused."

"Indeed," said Grossbard. "If Chester Kilsheimer doesn't want the world to know he's a pervert, I won't be the one to tell them."

Penny Claypool's eyes narrowed and, for an instant, he hoped she might revoke the honor so recently bestowed upon him. Alas, she merely wrinkled her nose, as though she'd tasted lemonade in need of sugar. "I'm glad we see eye to eye," she said. "Congratulations again! And I know I don't need to tell you this, Teddy, but remember to conduct yourself with the utmost integrity. You represent Hager Crossing now. You represent the Quince Pudding Festival." She embraced him a final time, crushing his shoulder against her bosom, and limped up the avenue.

This was the moment—as Grossbard recovered from the matron's hug—that the idea, as inspired as it was abominable, first dawned on him. Maybe the notion congealed in his thoughts because he was already thinking about the dog-luring letter and neighbors framing neighbors, or possibly it was that, as grand marshal, he would be above suspicion. Who could say? What mattered was that Grossbard drove to *The Double Crosser's* office that August morning feeling hopeless and dejected; he left armed with a nascent plot to burn down Findlay's office himself and to pin the crime on Palmer Quall.

XII

Once he'd recovered from his initial burst of excitement, Grossbard spent the next several days perfecting his scheme—mapping out every permutation and contingency in his mind. His mechanical work preparing his mother's house for sale afforded him ample opportunity to think matters through. He devoted hours to the logistics, factoring for every last detail and leaving nothing to chance. By the end of the week, he was confident that his plan would prove functional. It wasn't ethical, obviously. In fact, it was horrifically unethical. What amazed Grossbard, as he reflected on the moral implications of his scheme, was how little he actually cared.

After all, Lester Findlay was a depraved thief; shutting down his shoddy excuse for a news website would be a public service. And Palmer Quall—while he wasn't exactly a degenerate like Findlay, was the sort of man whose arrogance and ignorance made the world a decidedly worse place for those around him. Did this give Grossbard a right to see him jailed for a crime he hadn't committed? Possibly not. But with his own happiness—and Erica's—hanging in the balance, the psychiatrist was in no mood to be held back by moral niceties. Life was unfair: Grossbard had been born with unsightly teeth; his mother had suffered from a compulsive hoarding disorder; Palmer Quall had married the wrong woman and would now pay the consequences. At the end of the day, Grossbard decided, he could accept that.

The most challenging aspect of his plot, Grossbard discovered, was going about his everyday business as though nothing were out of the ordinary. To that end, he squandered an afternoon at the office of Feig & Rothschild Realtors, negotiating the details of the listing on his mother's house, and another full day obtaining estimates from an assortment of landscapers, plumbers, and electricians. The interior painting and papering he opted to do on his own—as much to keep himself busy as to save the expenditure. He also accompanied Penny Claypool to a bespoke tailor in Philadelphia to have Chester Kilsheimer's quince-colored tuxedo adjusted to his size. Between fixing up his mother's house and attending to the various minor duties that came with the title of grand marshal—such as autographing the "quince currency" used at the festival's carnival and writing his Quincentennial Address—Grossbard's days suddenly felt as hectic as they had previously seemed empty. Of course, once he'd hatched his own arson plot, the scheme never drifted far from his thoughts.

The first concrete step he took to effectuate his plan occurred two evenings before the opening Saturday of the festival. On the pretext of dropping off his latest column, Grossbard visited *The Double Crosser*'s office at the end of the workday; then he concealed himself in the men's restroom until the last staff members had departed. Alone in the dark, still office, he truly did feel like a criminal—but that didn't stop him.

Grossbard powered up the publisher's computer, logged into a fake email account that he'd created for the purpose, and sent Lester Findlay a message threatening to burn down his trailer. He did not sign the message "Palmer Quall"—he wasn't that foolish. Since he didn't have the technical sophistication to break into his rival's email account, he was banking on the authorities harnessing technology to trace the message back to the publisher's desktop. In order for that approach to work, he needed Findlay—and the police—to think that the sender had sought to remain anonymous.

The following night, shortly after sunset, Grossbard drove the eighty miles to the Delaware Landing Marina. As he'd hoped, the jetty stood deserted—not even a watchman in sight. *The Magic Bullet* rested in one of the farthest berths, bobbing ever so gently on the placid water, casting a black silhouette into the unknown. What a contrast, thought Grossbard, as he boarded the vessel, to the wild surf of the previous weekend. He didn't even need to rely on the railing for balance.

At the cabin, Grossbard encountered his only impediment: Quall, to the psychiatrist's surprise, had locked the hatch. He glanced around the deck, searching for an object that he might use to shatter the glass window of the wheelhouse; even if Erica's husband claimed the vessel had been burglarized, the coincidence of a break-in occurring the night before the fire would seem highly implausible. But then another stroke of good fortune befell Grossbard. On a whim, he glanced under the welcome mat at the foot of the gangway, and, sure enough, there lay a silver key. Twenty minutes later, he'd loaded a canister of Quall's smooth-burning Dutch fuel into the trunk of the Plymouth. Grossbard planned to abandon the container in Findlay's yard—a container that matched identically the one he'd left behind inside the publisher's boat.

When he returned home from the marina, he was too nervous to sleep. Instead, he penned his next column in advance. *Dear Vexed*, he wrote. *You're not the only person out there who despises his in-laws. Trust me on this. But when your wife says that they're your family too, she's dead wrong. Moreover, you write that your mother-in-law is sixty-two years old. That means she's had ample opportunity to plan ahead for a situation like this one. It is unfortunate that she cannot afford to pay her medical bills; however, lots of people cannot afford to pay their medical bills. You have no more moral obligation to your wife's mother than to any of these hapless strangers—after all, one of the cardinal rules of ethics is that all human lives have equal value. Ask yourself: If you start dishing out money now, when will it ever stop?*

The next morning, shortly after six o'clock, a quince-colored limousine arrived at Grossbard's doorstep to ferry him to the opening "quinceremonies."

XIII

The origins of the Quince Pudding festival had been lost to history, but a consensus among local authorities maintained that the nineteenth-century celebration had nothing to do with fruit. One outspoken antiquarian, a former village historian, insisted that the celebration took its name from a banquet to honor the presidency of John Quincy Adams. Another self-styled expert, the town's longtime reference librarian, argued that the event initially commemorated a local child who'd died of *quinsy*—an early term for an abscess of the tonsils—and that the quinces hadn't appeared until after World War I. According to Palmer Quall, who ran a front-page feature on the extravaganza, these "naysayers" had no inkling what they were talking about. "Everybody wants credit for a clever explanation," he penned in an editorial. "Sometimes, the simplest answer is correct. In this case, common sense dictates that the Quince Pudding Festival takes its name from the mouth-watering quince puddings prepared by the inhabitants of Hager Crossing." What Quall failed to mention—as was pointed out in dozens of letters that never saw print—was that quinces hadn't been grown in the region until the 1930s.

Although the celebration of "all things quince" lasted three weeks, the first Saturday featured the festival's two highlights. In the morning, a "Quincentennial" parade up Orchard Street was followed by the Pudding-Off; this year's taste test promised to be particularly competitive, as Penny Claypool had graciously retired from the competition to allow other "pud-diphiles" an opportunity to win. In the evening, a Quince Ball at the Congregational Church raised funds for disabled children. The three-hour window between these events afforded Grossbard just enough time to drive out to Camden Heights, burn Findlay's trailer, and return to deliver his speech. Who would ever think to question the alibi of the grand marshal, a man seen all day long in Hager Crossing and decked out in a quince color?

Grossbard's instincts told him that Lester Findlay, on the hunt for news and profit, would attend the opening. Another unexpected windfall also fell into the psychiatrist's lap. On the day before the festival, Palmer Quall had announced that the opening wasn't worth sacrificing a summer day on the cabin cruiser, so while his wife covered the parade and ball for *The Double Crosser*, the publisher planned to be trawling for bluefish *alone*. Never had the absence of an alibi seemed so perfect. Several minutes after Grossbard learned of this godsend from Erica, Penny Claypool said to him, "You must be the happiest man alive right now, Teddy," and he found himself in honest agreement—albeit for reasons that would have made the foundation-caked matron yearn for the era of Chester Kilsheimer.

From the moment his limousine arrived at the American Legion hall, which served as the Quince Committee's ad hoc nerve center, everything flowed smoothly. He rode through town on the lead float—a cylindrical structure shaped like a jelly jar—waving to the assortment of older, overweight tourists who lined the sidewalks. He kept his eyes peeled for Lester Findlay and was rewarded as they approached the local produce stands: the degenerate stood alone at the far end of the farmer's market, leaning against a wooden tent post, a cigarette dangling from his lips. When Grossbard waved in the man's direction, Findlay had the audacity to raise his middle finger. "I cannot fathom what I just saw," declared Penny Claypool. "Really. That man ought to be arrested." But a moment later, a troupe of Girl Scouts surrounded them for autographs, and all thoughts of prosecuting Lester Findlay was easily forgotten.

The Pudding-Off, an affair dominated by women over sixty, afforded Grossbard a few hours out of the limelight. He retreated to a shady, lightly trafficked area behind the grandstands, striving to appear inconspicuous in his quince-colored tux and fruit-fringed top hat. That's where Erica found him several minutes later. On any other day, he'd have been thrilled to see her—but with his arson only a few hours away, he felt too anxious for much conversation.

"I've been searching all over for you," she cried. His crush appeared truly ravishing in a strapless burgundy sundress that accentuated her pale skin. She inspected his hat more closely, and added, "Jesus. You look like Carmen Miranda."

"Thanks. That does wonders for my ego."

Erica smiled—but he sensed that she wasn't happy.

"So look, Ted, I need to speak with you."

"Fire away," he replied. "I'm free until noon."

Erica shifted her weight from one leg to the other. "I can't talk now—not here. Honestly, I've done something that I'm not proud of. Something terribly wrong."

"I'm sure it's not so awful," interjected Grossbard. "I know you pretty well, Erica Sucram. Do you remember when you said I didn't have it in me to kill? Well, you don't have it in you to do anything truly evil. I'm sure of it."

"I wish you were right," said Erica. "I don't know. Anyway, what I really need right now is your official blessing—as an ethicist. I know that sounds crazy, but if you tell me I'm not going to hell, it will mean a lot."

"You're not going to hell."

She shook her head—as though amused at the antics of a small child. "You have to hear what I've done first," she said. "But not now. If I don't start interviewing those pudding nuts, someone's going to get suspicious. How about between the awards presentation and the ball?"

"I can't," he objected, probably too quickly. "I'm promised to the quince folks all evening." As soon as the words left his mouth, he regretted them; she might easily seek him out later among the festival organizers, and find him AWOL.

"Please, Ted. Can't you sneak off for a moment?" She'd latched onto one of the giant yellow buttons of his jacket. "For me?"

"Not tonight. I'm sorry," he said. "How about tomorrow?"

Erica frowned, visibly annoyed. "Fine. I'll call you."

She released his coat and disappeared without even a goodbye. Not that it mattered, Grossbard assured himself. Tomorrow, after his drive to Camden Heights, Hager Corners would be an extremely different place.

XIV

The Pudding-Off ran into overtime. Three different puddings tied for first place, and while several board members wished to declare the confections to be co-equal among quinces, Penny Claypool reminded her colleagues that this would require them to reengrave the plaques. Instead, they asked Grossbard—as grand marshal—to render a final verdict. At first, he demurred. He didn't particularly like quince pudding, to be candid, or quinces in general, and when he'd sampled the trio earlier, they'd all tasted more or less the same. Yet when it became clear that any resistance on his part would only delay the inevitable, and his trip to Camden Heights, he selected one of the puddings—randomly—and placed a garland of quince blossoms on the gray-tufted head of the winner. Another hour elapsed while he listened to the afternoon's keynote speaker, a botanist from New York City named Arnold Brinkman, deliver a rather tedious lecture on "The Quince and American Democracy." The sun had already dipped below the tree line when he finally set out for Camden Heights. He had only an hour to spare until nine o'clock, when the ball was slated to begin.

Grossbard drove cautiously, careful not to draw police attention. He'd donned a pair of latex hospital gloves to avoid leaving behind fingerprints. He'd also changed into his street clothes—only a fool would commit arson dressed in a yellow-green tuxedo—and, on the trip to the CrossConnect trailer, he perspired through his shirt. Every artery in his body felt charged with a live electrical wire. *What am I doing?* he kept asking himself. *I'm committing a felony. I could go to prison.* But none of these thoughts managed to override his intense dislike for Lester Findlay and Palmer Quall. *Don't think too much, Ted*, he said aloud. *Act today, think tomorrow.* And he did.

His enemy's block appeared largely deserted. Iron grates covered the front doors of the funeral parlor, while the entrance to the pool hall stood around the corner, its parking lot protected by a chain-link and barbed-wire fence. Other than the pulsing flash of neon from the side street, Findlay's house stood shrouded in nearly complete darkness. A cat scurried away as Grossbard climbed the cinderblock steps, followed by another feline, this one lame, shambling on a damaged paw.

As the psychiatrist had anticipated, the trailer entrance was locked—and, this time, he couldn't even find a welcome mat. His initial plan had been to fracture a window and pour the gasoline inside, but he discovered that one of Findlay's back panes was already broken. Grossbard hoisted the fuel canister onto his shoulder and poured its contents through the hole. Next, he lit a match and tossed it onto the trailer carpet, where it connected with the accelerant. Magic. As he raced back to his vehicle, he tossed the can—already dusted for prints—onto Findlay's lawn.

An hour later, while firefighters struggled with a five-alarm blaze that ultimately enveloped Findlay's home and the pool hall, Grossbard spoke to the leading citizens of Hager Crossing on the importance of leading moral lives. All agreed—with the exception of Chester Kilsheimer's sister—that Grossbard's speech was the most distinguished Quincentennial Address in the history of the festival.

XV

Grossbard logged onto his computer the next morning and was greeted by the headline he'd waited for all summer. The front page of the *Laurendale Ledger* read:

Fire Guts X-Connect
Arson Suspected; Police Follow Leads

Similar stories appeared on the websites of the *Camden Heights Clarion* and the *Burlington County Times*. Even the *Philadelphia Inquirer* carried a small item about the fire—on the same page where it reported on the Quince Pudding Festival. The CrossConnect website was entirely unavailable.

The *Ledger* article quoted Lester Findlay as saying, "I've been receiving anonymous threats, but they're anonymous only in name. I know who's been sending them." He did not identify his enemy to the media, but Grossbard had little doubt he'd report Parker Quall to the authorities. Meanwhile, all Grossbard had to do was wallpaper his mother's bathroom and let justice take its course. He considered phoning Erica, but fearing that might appear suspicious, he waited for her call. To his dismay, he did not hear from her that Sunday or on Monday. On Tuesday, as he was contemplating a visit to *The Double Crosser*'s office, the doorbell rang.

Two Camden Heights police officers waited on his mother's front porch. Only at that moment did it strike Grossbard that he might himself be a suspect—that Findlay could have given his name, along with Quall's, to the police. In a flood of panic, he considered fleeing. But to where? And how would he survive? Even as he contemplated a life on the lam, he knew his only realistic option was to try his luck with the authorities.

The older of the pair introduced himself as Detective April—"like the rainy month." The younger shared a long, Greek-sounding name that Grossbard didn't quite catch. Grossbard had no choice but to invite them into his mother's living room. Drop cloths covered the upholstery, so he retrieved two hard-backed chairs from the kitchen for the officers. "I'm painting," he apologized, settling onto the edge of his mother's piano bench. "If I'd been expecting you . . . "

"Quite alright," said April. "We won't take up much of your time."

Grossbard sensed the adrenaline coursing into his veins. He held his hands firmly behind his back—fearful that they might reveal a tremor. The white sun of morning crept around the curtains, casting dark patches on the carpet.

"You look nervous," said the Greek cop, removing a notepad from his belt.

"Exhausted," answered Grossbard. "I'm the grand marshal in the Quince Pudding Festival."

"How's that going?"

"Good enough. Busy," said Grossbard. He decided that the appearance of candor might help his case, so he added, "The only problem is that I don't like quinces."

"Grand Marshal in the Quince Pudding Festival," echoed the younger cop, "and he doesn't like quinces. That's just genius."

"It is rather ironic," said Grossbard. "Even I can see that."

"Anyway," said the older cop, "we're not going to make you eat any quinces. What we're here to discuss is Saturday night's fire. I imagine you've heard about it."

"Only what's in the newspapers."

"I should hope so," said the younger cop.

"What we want to know, in particular, is whether you have any insights you want to share about this incident," continued the older cop. "For example, anybody you can think of who might want to put the CrossConnect editors out of business?"

Grossbard paused, as though thinking. "Not a soul."

"You're certain? Not even Palmer Quall?"

Now Grossbard waited even longer before answering. To his delight, the officers exchanged a telling look.

"I'm positive Palmer had nothing to do with this," he finally said. "I imagine you're asking me about Palmer because of that time he threatened to burn down Lester Findlay's office. But that was idle chatter. Palmer's a big talker—but he wouldn't hurt a fly. He doesn't have it in him."

That led to a series of additional inquiries regarding his publisher, his publisher's attitude toward his competitors, even the last time he'd seen Palmer Quall in person. After thirty minutes of friendly interrogation, the young officer closed his notebook and shook Grossbard's hand. "One more question, Dr. Grossbard," said the detective—almost as an after-thought. "Where were you on Saturday evening?"

"Me? I was at the Quince Pudding Festival," answered Grossbard. "I had to judge the Pudding-Off and then I gave a speech."

The officers thanked him for his time.

Later that evening, watching the television news, Grossbard learned that Palmer Quall had been arrested for aggravated arson and reckless endangerment. A state magistrate set bail at $2 million.

XVI

Grossbard met Erica for lunch at the Star-Crossed Café the following Monday. She'd phoned early in the morning, after a week of silence, sounding more shell-shocked than desperate. When she arrived at the eatery, rather than wearing one of the revealing cotton dresses that drew occasional catcalls around the business district, she sported an oversized black T-shirt and sweatpants. "Sorry I'm late," she apologized, sliding into a corner booth. "I had to stop by the office to hand out pink slips." She glanced over the menu before pushing it aside. "That reminds me—so I don't forget. This Friday will be the final edition of *The Double Crosser*, which means we won't need any more ethics columns. If you'd like, I can recommend you to some of the editors I know in Trenton."

"That won't be necessary," replied Grossbard. "I don't care about the column one way or another. But isn't this all a bit sudden?" He leaned forward, determined to play the part of devoted childhood friend. "I mean: I know things look grim right now, but maybe Palmer will be acquitted."

"It doesn't matter. Findlay will still crush us," said Erica. "How long do you think it will take him to get a new website up and running? A few weeks?" She shook her head decisively. "Besides, I'm through with the newspaper business, at least for the present. Quite frankly, Teddy, I'm ready for a change."

"You must be devastated."

He kept his tone steady and sympathetic. Now that Palmer Quall was stewing in the Burlington County jail, he had no intention of screwing up his prospects.

"That's the awful part," said Erica. "I'm not devastated. *I'm happy.*"

Erica flashed him a smile, at once sheepish and sweet. For a brief moment, he felt the satisfaction of believing she shared his feelings—but her smile vanished quickly, taking with it his sense of promise.

"You're going to think I'm an awful person," said Erica, "but I've been seeing someone behind Palmer's back. Or *seeing* might be too strong a word—I've only actually *seen* him twice. He lives in Baltimore. But I've been speaking to him every day for the past month." She spoke rapidly, obviously self-conscious. "The truth is that I've been wanting out for some time now. I didn't want things to end this way, of course—and I won't entirely abandon Palmer if he needs financial help—but as far as marriage goes, we're through. As soon as I close up *The Double Crosser*, I'm going to throw caution to the wind and move to Maryland."

To say that Grossbard was dumbfounded would be an understatement. One of Erica's greatest selling points, after all, had been her loyalty—even to a man like Palmer Quall. That she would abandon the man so rapidly, even if he were an imbecile, disturbed Grossbard's sense of justice and fair play.

"Please, Ted. Say something," said Erica. "Anything."

"I'm at a loss," he said.

"I know you must think I'm a terrible person. But you have to understand how difficult it was being married to Palmer. Honestly, when I found out what he'd done, I wasn't the slightest bit surprised. I guess, deep down, I knew he was capable of something like this all along."

Part of Grossbard resented her betrayal—of her husband, of him. Yet the romantic strategist in his psyche reminded him that Erica's new relationship was destined to fail and that now was the moment to position himself for the rebound.

"I don't think you're a terrible person," said Grossbard, measuring each word with care. "It's just a lot to digest at once."

"So you really don't hate me?"

"Of course, I don't *hate* you," answered Grossbard. "I don't even think you're a terrible person. I think you're a good person in a terrible situation."

An expression of genuine relief crossed Erica's features.

"I'm so glad," she said. "It's your fault anyway."

"My fault?"

"At least partly." Erica looked more cheerful now. "Do you remember when you asked me about Todd Serspinksi?"

"The hockey player with no neck?"

"I think he has a sexy neck, just so you know," said Erica. "Well, I hadn't thought of him in years, but when you mentioned his name, I couldn't resist looking him up online, and one thing led to another." She paused as though searching his face for approval. "Todd coaches college now. Division III, but still."

"I'm sure you'll be very happy together," he said.

At the end of their lunch, when Grossbard hugged her, Erica promised that she'd keep him posted on her new life. He suspected that she'd try, at least for a while. He also knew that he'd never speak to her again.

XVII

That was Ted Grossbard's final week in Hager Crossing. He hired a contractor to finish the painting and wallpapering, unwilling to spend anymore time in the town than absolutely necessary. Even Penny Claypool's pleas—and later, recriminations—could not induce him to remain for the closing ceremonies of the Quince Pudding Festival. The only person to whom he said goodbye, before driving back to New York City, was his mother's elderly neighbor, Mr. Berg.

"I'll miss having you around and I'll miss your columns too, Theodore," said Berg. "Sis and I always said you were a good kid. Ugly as sin, we said. But a heart of gold." The old man appeared to think he'd paid Grossbard a great compliment; he shook his hand vigorously, then patted him on the back before strolling away.

Once he'd returned to Manhattan and started his new job at the state forensic facility, Grossbard made a point not to follow the trial of Palmer Quall. In fact, after the publisher's conviction, he kept himself willingly ignorant of the man's sentence. The less he found out, Grossbard knew, the less he had to second-guess.

The psychiatrist did check up on Lester Findlay's revived ethics column now and then—mostly to remind himself that, by comparison to the conman, he was a saint. Once enough time had passed, Grossbard even sent CrossConnect an anonymous letter. He asked: *Let's say I framed a romantic rival for a serious criminal offense—and he's now serving a long prison sentence. My romance didn't pan out after all, and there's presently no benefit to me from keeping this innocent man in prison. What should I do?*

Grossbard was amused to see that the degenerate ran his note, and answered: *Turn yourself in, dammit! Crime never pays.*

He ignored the conman's advice. In the first place, Findlay didn't know a damn thing about ethics. And even if, in this particular case, Dr. Ethics turned out to be right, being right wasn't everything. Sometimes, the path to morality loomed clear, but a man chose not to follow it. Grossbard decided this would be such a case, and knowing that no human being is perfect, he put the tragedy behind him and carried on with his life.

About the Author

Jacob M. Appel is a physician, attorney, and bioethicist in New York City, where he teaches at the Mount Sinai School of Medicine. His publications include four novels and seven collections of stories. He is the winner of numerous awards, including the Hudson Prize, the Dundee International Book Prize, the Robert Watson Literary Prize, and the Devil's Kitchen Reading Award. Learn more at jacobmappel.com.